Scar Bonds: The Scars that Bind Us

Quirk of Fates Shorts #4

By Lisa Oliver

Scar Bonds: The Scars That Bind Us – Quirk of Fates Shorts #4

Copyright © Lisa Oliver, 2025

ALL RIGHTS RESERVED

Cover Design by Lisa Oliver

Background and cover images – Shutterstock.com

First Edition February 2025

All rights reserved under the International and Pan-American Conventions. No part of this book may be reproduced or transmitted in any form or by any means, electronic or mechanical including photocopying, recording or by any information storage or retrieval system, without permission in writing from the author, Lisa Oliver. Yoursintuitively@gmail.com

No part of this book may be scanned, uploaded, or distributed via the internet or any other means, electronic or print, without permission from Lisa Oliver. **Warning:** The unauthorized reproduction or distribution of this copyrighted work is illegal. Criminal copyright infringement, including infringement without monetary gain, is investigated by the FBI and is punishable by up to **5 years in federal prison and a fine of $250,000**. Please purchase only authorized electronic or print editions and do not participate in or encourage the electronic piracy of copyrighted material. Your support of the author's rights and livelihood is appreciated.

Scar Bonds: The Scars that Bind Us is a work of fiction. Names, characters, places, and incidents are either the product of the author's imagination or are used fictitiously and any resemblance to any actual persons, living or dead, events or locales is entirely coincidental. All trademarks are owned by the relevant companies and are used for reference purposes in this book only.

Table of Contents

Chapter One 7
Chapter Two 18
Chapter Three 27
Chapter Four 33
Chapter Five 43
Chapter Six 62
Chapter Seven 77
Chapter Eight 92
Chapter Nine 112
Chapter Ten 125
Chapter Eleven 139
Chapter Twelve 151
Chapter Thirteen 163
Chapter Fourteen 176
Chapter Fifteen 188
Chapter Sixteen 203
Epilogue 211
About the Author 218
Other Books By Lisa Oliver 220

Dedication

From my heart to yours, my friends,

Hug the ones you love,

LOVE WINS

Author's Note

The Quirk of Fates Short series are not meant to be in-depth stories, but rather a quick look at what can happen when the Fates are determined to have their own way and bring couples together in unusual or random ways.

Each book is completely standalone and covers the meeting and mating of individual couples. Sometimes, even the worlds are different – in some, paranormals are known about publicly, and in others they might not be. In this case, paranormals are public about who they are although that doesn't always make things easier for them, lol.

I truly hope you enjoy Senan and Finlay's story.

Thank you,

Lisa xx

Chapter One

"I don't understand why Jeffrey insisted on booking this event. It's insane."

Senan glanced at his friend Gabby, before carefully wiping off lipstick stains from a glass before placing it in the dishwasher tray. He rubbed the mark from his rubber gloves, rinsed them, and picked up and checked the rim of the next glass. Lipstick almost never came off in the dishwasher alone which was why Senan was hand-checking and rinsing sixty glasses after the luncheon event.

"What's wrong with the next event?" Senan was tired. His wings wanted a stretch, and that was impossible to do in his button-up shirt. "Please tell me it's not tonight." It was already getting close to three, and if they had another event to do that evening it meant he wouldn't be getting to bed until after midnight.

"It *is* tonight. Don't you keep an eye on the schedule?"

"Why should I, when I know you'll do that for me." Senan flashed a quick smile at his friend before checking the last of the glasses. "What horrors do we have to contend with this time?" *So much for sleep.* He suppressed a yawn.

"The leaders of the Luna Pack are hosting a dinner for the paranormal group leaders from the *entire state*." Gabby's voice rose up at the end of the sentence. "Eighty-four adults are expected to attend, with a sit-down dinner, blah, blah, blah. No wonder Masie was freaking out that the lady's garden club luncheon took so long. There're six courses."

"Sounds normal for a paranormal event." Senan was thankful that his voice didn't shake, although his body froze just hearing the word "paranormal". There was a time when the mention of the Luna Pack would send him into the darkness for days.

He opened the dishwasher and carefully slid the now full tray of glasses into it.

"It's the rules Jeffrey has posted on this sheet that makes me want to scream." Gabby's voice rose again, but then one of the things Senan loved about his friend was her erratic personality. "Listen to this. Apparently, this applies to all attending staff. No makeup. No colognes or perfumes. No scented deodorants..."

"Shifters have sensitive noses." Senan flicked the switch on the dishwasher, let out the sink full of hot water he'd been working at, and then stripped off his rubber gloves.

"I understand that, but that's not all Jeffrey had to say." Gabby snorted. "The Luna Pack Alpha, who is apparently hosting this event, is insistent that staff representing the Gourmet Outsourced company will not be distracting to their guests in any way. Accordingly all staff will have their hair tied back, refrain from wearing jewelry, cover any tattoos, and ensure that the only clothing they are wearing fully adheres to the company's strict dress code."

"Covering tattoos will be difficult without makeup. You'll have to wear a long-sleeved shirt." Senan leaned his butt against the edge of the sink, smiling at his friend.

When Senan met Gabby two years before, after securing a job as a waiter and general kitchen hand at the Gourmet Outsourced company, his first thought was "explosive." Everything about Gabby was larger than life, from her mop of bright red hair that fell around her face in waves that seemed to defy gravity in the way it flew around in every direction, to her numerous freckles that covered most of her nose and cheeks, and yes, her very brightly colored tattoos – ink that covered almost her entire body.

Gabby was as fun as she appeared, and never took anything seriously except her friendships. She had pretty much adopted Senan from his very first day, something he was truly grateful for. She didn't know he was one of the paranormals he avoided like the plague – no one he worked with did – and yet she was staunchly loyal and protective of him. Senan had thought about telling her a dozen times… but that could lead to him revealing some parts of his life he'd never wanted anyone to know. It was far easier to glamour himself and appear human every time he had to work.

"I'm not on the list to attend," Gabby flicked at the piece of paper taped to the prep room bulletin board in disgust. "Jeffrey claims in his instruction sheet that any member of staff that is considered striking or distinctive in looks – he actually used the word striking – would not be eligible to work the event. The Alpha has specifically stated he only wants non-descript, quiet, and efficient staff tending to his guests. It's like he wants the staff to blend into the wallpaper."

Senan quickly covered his yawn with his hand. "Sounds exactly like an Alpha wolf decree to me. But why are you reading that rubbish if you're not expected to work tonight? I already know Jeffrey wouldn't have scheduled me for a paranormal event." It was the one thing Senan insisted on in his contract, before he'd even been offered the job.

"I'm spouting all this shit because you're on the list." Gabby poked the offending piece of paper. "I apparently don't blend into the wallpaper enough. Who knew?"

She spread her arms and twirled around, making Senan smile even as the pit of lead in his stomach grew. But she was back at the pinned piece of paper soon enough. "I know you have a paranormal aversion, I don't know why, and it's not my business.

You do you. But you're listed to work the tables tonight with Aisha, Fern, Alex, and Wyatt." She tapped the names on the list as she read them off.

"That has to be a mistake." Senan reached into his pocket for his phone. "Jeffrey was clearly rushed when he did this and just put the wrong name down." He tapped Jeffrey's contact on his phone, hearing it ring.

"Jeffrey's at that kink conference all weekend," Gabby said quietly. "Not even his mother will be able to get hold of him until Monday."

"It's not a kink conference, it's a beginner Shibari course. I forgot, darn it." Senan sighed as he disconnected the call and put his phone away. "I just won't go. I can't. With any luck Jeffrey will have learned enough from the course to be in a good mood on Monday when he learns about me ducking out on an event."

"You're team leader, you can't back out." Gabby's face was clearly designed to tug at Senan's people-pleaser genes. Not that he had any, but she was difficult to ignore. "Think about it. Aisha is going to be shitting kittens around all that Alpha testosterone. I can't think why Jeffrey included her in the first place. Fern and Alex will be okay, but Wyatt is another one who gets easily distracted. I'm guessing that's why Jeffrey wants you there. You can't just abandon them in their hour of need."

"Isn't that just a tad dramatic, even for you?" Senan rubbed his chin. Unfortunately, for all her flair, Gabby was right. If he was listed as team leader, then the others would be depending on him, and it wasn't as though he could come up with a credible excuse so quickly. *Although...* "Who's doing the prep and clean up?" Senan asked as he had another idea.

"Brennan." Gabby frowned. "Do you think that's where Jeffrey made the fuck up? Brennan can serve just as well as you can."

"Exactly, my lovely friend." Feeling immediately better, Senan rushed over, hugging her quickly before letting go, and reaching for his phone again. "I'll let Brennan know he's serving tonight, and I'll run the team from the prep area which means I don't have to interact with any paranormal at all."

"Are you ever going to tell me how you got this?" Gabby's bright red fingernail lightly touched Senan's scar – the scar that ran from the corner of his eye right down to his mouth. His friend had no idea how bad it looked without the glamour. "That has to be a paranormal incident."

"I'm not saying anything because that business is in the past and I've got to plan for tonight. But as always, my wonderful friend, you've reminded me of the excuse I'll have ready for Jeffrey on Monday if he complains about what I've done. Paranormals find scars distracting as much as unnatural scents so I'm simply adhering to his rules, and considering he should never have rostered me on tonight for this event anyway, he can't make a fuss." Senan gave Gabby a truly wide smile. "I do love it when a plan comes together."

"Message me when you get home," Gabby insisted. "I'll be the one sitting curled up on my couch with my cat, munching my way through a tub of ice cream as I drool over Maximus Khan."

"The tiger shifter?" Senan was very familiar with Gabby's type. They'd watched more than a few movies together in the past. "Has he got a new movie out?"

"Nope. I rewatch the old ones, which is even better. I know exactly when to pause the screen for the good bits.

When he rips his shirt off I get shivers all over." Gabby hugged herself with a wide grin.

"Yes, well, you'll have to get the shivers for both of us." Senan looked at his screen, finding Brennan's contact details. A shirtless Maximus Khan, a notable paranormal movie star, was enough to make anyone's body shiver and their knees go weak. It was tempting to join Gabby on her couch and drool over shirtless paranormals from afar, but Senan had responsibilities. "Come on Brennan, answer your darn phone."

Chapter Two

"What are you doing here?" Finlay groaned as he spotted his brother, Morgan, who appeared at his bedroom door completely unexpectedly. "I've been away a week. I'm tired, grubby, and all I want to do is head out for a shift." He checked that his rifle was unloaded, set it carefully in its case, flicked the double locks, and stowed the locked case into his gun safe. He yawned as he glanced at his brother again.

"I sometimes wish I'd never given you a key," he added as he unclipped the holster for the knife on his thigh, took two more blades out of his boots, and laid them on his bedside cabinet. Finlay glanced at his brother. "Yes, I have noticed you're all dressed up. Don't tell me, you've finally landed yourself a date for the night. That would make a change from you burying your nose in profit and loss statements, policy documents, and spreadsheets."

"I stopped by to pick you up," Morgan said tersely. "It's good I came early because as per normal, you're not ready."

"Pick me up for what? The last time we double-dated we almost came to blows, and our dates left, leaving both of us with hard dicks and nowhere to put them. I don't know about you, but I have no desire to repeat that scenario even if it was ten years ago. And it's not like you need me to hold your hand or give you bullet points on how to conduct yourself in public." Finlay pulled his shirt over his head and tossed it in the general direction of his laundry hamper.

"In case you didn't hear me the first time," he added as he stretched. "I'm tired, dirty, and stressed to the max. My wolf needs to stretch his legs, I have a desperate need to eat something that doesn't come wrapped in plastic, and then I plan to sleep for at least two days. I have confidence in you. Anything you have to attend you can do without me."

"It's the annual Paranormal Collective dinner – the event our pack..."

"Your pack," Finlay corrected automatically. "You're the Alpha of the Luna Pack, not me. Never me."

"Don't be too sure. Regardless." If Morgan's jaw tightened any further, he'd have wicked dentist bills. "You promised me you would attend if I couldn't find a suitable plus one. As I couldn't find a suitable plus one, and as you're the only person I trust to watch my back..."

Finlay's shoulders slumped. "You seriously don't fight fair, did you know that? And I'll bet you a steak dinner you didn't even look for a date. You spend far too much time at your desk or fielding complaints from your pack members." Resigning himself the inevitable, Finley sat on the bed, unlaced his boots, and kicked them off before standing and unbuttoning his pants, shoving them down his legs.

"Give me five minutes. I'll have to clean up, or I'll be doing nothing but offending a dozen important noses at this event of yours. Grab a drink from the bar in the living room if you want a head start on what promises to be a boring evening."

Not looking to see if his brother followed his suggestion or not, Finlay stalked into his ensuite bathroom, turning the shower on with such a wrench the handle almost came off in his hand. As he stepped under the water, not even waiting for it to heat up, he took deep breaths, trying to calm both himself and his wolf. He was genuinely running on fumes, and the last thing he felt like doing was being sociable.

It wasn't Morgan's fault. Finlay knew that. He and his brother had been born five minutes apart, and Morgan, who had appeared first, had the good luck – or bad depending on who was talking about it – to be named the Alpha-heir when he was only twelve and shifted for the first time. Finlay was always the "spare". He knew it, the pack knew it, and honestly, Finlay wouldn't want Morgan's job for anything.

No one expected their father - the Luna Pack Alpha Morgan was named after - to die in a freak lightning strike. One of their father's quirks was to run in wolf form in a thunderstorm. Finlay remembered him saying years before how running with the wind gave their father an adrenaline rush that nothing else could rival. Until he didn't run fast enough.

When she heard the news of her mate's death, their mother - the Alpha mate - patted Morgan on his shoulder and kissed Finlay on his cheek, before disappearing into her bedroom where she was found dead three days later. The fated mate bond could be both a blessing and a curse.

Morgan became Alpha of the Luna Pack – his life changing in just one day. Finlay stuck around the pack for a couple of months, helping his brother adjust as much as he could before a couple of pack members started making rumblings that the pack had two Alphas, and it was causing dissent. After a brief chat with his brother, where they both agreed it was necessary, Finlay packed his bags, left the pack house and hadn't looked back.

But it's never that easy to let go, Finlay thought as he washed himself off. Finlay was the only family Morgan had left, and until Morgan found himself a mate and had a few pups of his own, Finlay was also the pack Alpha-heir. Even though Finlay had built a life of his own that had nothing to do with the pack, Morgan clearly meant it when he said Finlay was the only one he could trust to watch his back. Finlay was so worried that he'd end up as the Alpha of their family pack, he'd take a bullet for his brother.

I'd rather take a fucking bullet now than have to schmooze and talk nice to a bunch of clan, coven, and pride leaders. Leaving the bathroom well before he was ready, Finlay barely dried himself completely before he was back in the bedroom.

He quickly pulled out his suit, thankful he must've taken the time to get it cleaned at some point since he'd worn it last. His shirt collar was too tight, and Finlay gave up trying to get the top button closed, and left it open, quickly knotting a tie loosely over it. Shrugging on his jacket, Finlay left that unbuttoned as well and sat on the bed so he could put his boots back on.

"I'll do," he muttered as he checked his reflection in the mirror. Tired, dark eyes stared back at him as he flicked a comb through his shoulder-length blond hair.

Striding into the living room, Finlay frowned when he noticed the half-empty bottle of whiskey on the bar counter. He was sure it'd been unopened before Morgan had gotten to it. "Is everything all right?"

"Yep." Morgan chucked back the rest of the drink in his glass and set it carefully on the counter. He met Finlay's eyes and Finlay realized his brother was as tired and stressed as he was feeling. "I swear if one more person says, 'We didn't do things like that in your father's day' I'll slash their throat and to hell with the consequences."

"You need to get laid," Finlay said quickly. "Come on, you can drive me. Are there going to be any potential bond mates for you at this event of yours?"

"If you hear the elders speak, there are three possibilities that they consider suitable. If you're asking me, not a one."

"You can tell me about them on the way, not that I can offer much in the way of an opinion," Finlay said, taking his brother's arm that seemed to be reaching for the whiskey bottle again. "However, the sooner we get there, the sooner it will be over, and you can go back to your desk, and I can get some wolf time."

Finlay wasn't sure what to think when Morgan didn't reply – *he must be in a real funk*. But at least he let Finlay tug him from the room as they headed out to the car.

Chapter Three

"You're doing great Aisha, just get those last two plates out to the table and then there's just clean up to do. Wyatt, if you and Alex can roll out the dessert carts, and leave them for the guests to help themselves, that would be excellent. Brennan and Fern I'll leave you two to organize the coffee table – just make sure there is plenty of everything any of the guests might need. Thank you all."

Two hours into the event, Senan was quietly confident things had been going as well as they could be considering he was flinching with every strange noise or the moment anyone came close to the door of the prep area. His magic was acutely tuned to the fact he was less than a hundred yards from predators – predators who didn't like or appreciate people like him. It made for a nervous time, even though the other servers were doing a great job at the tables, so it wasn't as though any of the guests were looking for someone to complain to.

The chef, Maisie, and her team were amazing, as always. The event had a preplanned menu, so there were no issues with people getting the wrong foods. All of the food prep had been done quickly, and without any fuss. None of the waiters had dropped a plate, or spilled any food when serving, and Senan simply reminded them before every course to be unobtrusive and not to engage in conversation.

The event guests seemed to be having a great time, if the noise coming from the dining room was any indication. There were very few raised voices. That was one advantage of a paranormal event where everyone had excellent hearing, although Senan's skin still shivered every time he thought he heard a deep voice getting closer to the prep area where he was now taking care of clean up.

"Did you need a hand with those glasses?" Aisha came back into the prep area, her face flushed. "The last of the plates have gone out."

Senan checked the list of instructions that came with every event. "Apparently the guests will be leaving the dining area once they've all finished eating and will be conducting their actual meeting in another room, so you can collect dirty plates then." He caught the redness of Aisha's face and waved at the table. "Sit down. Did anyone give you any trouble? You're looking a little stressed. Don't worry about these glasses, I can finish them myself, but thank you."

"Thanks, and it's okay, no one gave me any trouble." Aisha plopped down in a seat with a whoosh. "It's a bit strange having no one pay any attention to you at all when you're leaning past them putting plates on the table, but now I'm thinking about it, that really wasn't a bad thing. At least no one was pinching my butt or asking for my number. No" - she sighed – "it's just that I'm not getting a lot of sleep. I've got exams coming up soon, and so I've been studying every spare minute I can keep my eyes open."

Senan was grateful for Aisha's chatter as she kept up a steady stream of words about her studies, her deadbeat boyfriend that she absolutely was going to dump as soon as she had a spare five minutes, and some random story about a friend of hers who thought she might be pregnant. Wyatt and Alex came in, taking other spare seats, and by the time Brennan and Fern came in to let him know that the first of the guests were starting to leave, Senan had finished the glasses and most of the plates.

"That's great to hear. If you want to just go out there and clean off the tables... You know the drill. I'll take care of the last of the dishes, and we should be done in thirty minutes or so."

"Sounds good to me," Brennan said, standing up and stretching. "I have a date tonight. Totally thrilled you took my stint at the sink, by the way, Senan. I didn't want to turn up and be touching my lady with dishwasher hands." He waved them in the air as the others laughed.

"That's why I wear gloves." Senan smiled as he turned back to the sink mentioned. There were still the dessert course plates to be washed and stacked, not to mention glasses, cutlery... Eighty people eating made for a lot of dishes so the next thirty minutes would be busy.

Senan thought longingly of his small house. Once he walked through his front door, he had the whole weekend to himself. *Two whole days where I can smell like me, look like me, and just be me, wings and all. I've just got to get through the next hour until I get home.*

As far as Senan was concerned that couldn't come quickly enough. Suppressing his scent was magically draining for him, and he'd already been tired before his second event of the day started. But the scent suppressor was working, and at a paranormal event, that was the most important thing of all. *Not long to go now.*

Chapter Four

Finlay felt his brain was being tugged in all directions and he couldn't wait for the evening to be over. The most important thing, according to Morgan, was being hospitable to their guests, and as far as Finlay was concerned, he'd done that.

The food served by discreet staff was wholesome and cooked exactly to any discerning paranormal's specifications. The catering company had clearly used organic ingredients, heavily meat-based, and the meat that had been served was only lightly seasoned, and, in most cases, barely cooked. Perfect in other words. So there was nothing to upset any of the guests.

Finlay knew most of the attendees already, so it wasn't as though conversation was an issue. Not that there was much of that going on either – shifters preferred to eat and then talk.

It stemmed from wolf shifter lore that stated if an Alpha ate with someone, it meant they didn't intend on killing that person – at least that day. The meal was a gesture of friendship so to speak, but no serious topics would be discussed until after the meal was done.

It appeared the leading vampire in the room, Lord Falcon, and his coven members remembered that unspoken rule from the previous year's events and kept their chatter to in between courses.

So, everything was good on the event side of things. Morgan should be happy about that. But it's what he'd said in the car on the way to the event that was bothering Finlay more than he could let on.

"I'm thinking of stepping down and leaving the pack." The words fell like a knife between them. Morgan had barely gotten the car out of the driveway before he just blurted them out.

"Gods, you seriously are in a funk, aren't you? You can't leave the pack." Finlay said the first words that came into his head. "You're the Alpha. Dad chose you as heir and you trained to be in that position for years before he died. It's all you've ever wanted."

"It is what I wanted." Morgan sounded almost savage, although Finlay wondered if his brother's anger was more internally directed than meant for him. "But that was back when I thought I was a decent man. When I believed I could rule the pack with honor, and make our father proud. That's all I've ever wanted to do."

Now Finlay was confused. "What the hell changed then? You do all that and more. I know you think the elders are on your case about mating and all that, but if you remember Dad used to complain about them, too. Just remind them you're the Alpha and get them to back off. Tell them you're waiting for your Fated Mate and refuse to listen if they keep harping on about it."

"I won't get a Fated Mate." Now Morgan sounded bitter. "People who do cruel things to innocents don't get to meet the one fated for them. That's not how it works."

Cruel? Finlay didn't understand it. If anything, Morgan was too nice, which was why he didn't tell the pack elders to just back off and leave him alone. "Don't do anything rash," he said quickly as he saw they were drawing up to the convention center. "You've been under a lot of stress, and I haven't been helping as much as I should have. We'll talk, yeah? Get this business tonight over and done with, and after I've had some sleep, I'll come over, and we can chat. Or you can come to mine if you think it'll be more private there. I'm sure we can work something out."

Morgan had just snorted, and as Lord Falcon and his entourage had been waiting for them in the parking lot it wasn't as though Finlay could say anything else. The moment Morgan stepped out of the car he was the Alpha their father had raised him to be – smiling politely but not too effusively, reminding those attending he was the ruler of the biggest paranormal group for miles around, in a subtle way Finlay had never been able to pull off.

So there was that, and the worry of being left a pack he had no idea how to run, or inclination, should've been enough. But there was something else tingling Finlay's wolf senses, and as Finlay relied on his wolf for his life and had done on more than one occasion, he went through the motions of eating and conversing, trying to filter through the sensations coming through his senses. Something... or someone was getting his wolf in a tizzy.

But who and why? Finlay wasn't perceiving any threat. The guests were all friends as much as powerful paranormals could be when they all came together, and his wolf wasn't picking up on any negative vibes from anyone.

The staff wasn't ringing any alarm bells either. The two women were nervous, but that was understandable. All non-paras with an ounce of preservation would feel that way in a room full of Alpha figures. The male servers were just as nervous, quiet and efficient. Finlay watched one of them a few times – his nameplate said "Wyatt." But again, it seemed Wyatt was just easily distracted. But he put his plates down without spilling anything and his colleague, someone called Brennan, only had to nudge him a few times.

So if it wasn't the staff and it wasn't the guests, then who? The cooking staff belonging to the catering company had all left when he and Morgan arrived. The head chef had introduced the wait staff, and yet...

There has to be someone else with them. Someone who hasn't been introduced. Why?

Finlay watched the staff in between the courses, keeping a half an ear on his brother, making polite chit chat when spoken to but not engaging more than necessary. His behavior wouldn't be considered unusual. Morgan was always known as the more outgoing brother, and the Alpha as host was playing his part perfectly despite the bombshell he'd dropped in the car.

He got his first clue as to the other person when one of the serving ladies went through into the prep room. The door was only open a moment, but Finlay distinctly heard a male voice speaking to her. He quickly scanned the room, but all three male servers and the other female one were still tending to tables.

All through the courses, Finlay only heard the voice twice more. Both times, it was as if the sound resonated with something deep inside of him – it definitely perked up his wolf, but not in a threatening sort of a way. It was more like a puzzle Finlay was itching to solve, a present he wanted to unwrap.

"Did you want to take a coffee through with you to the meeting?" Morgan asked as the last of the food was eaten. "We're about ready to go through to the other room." The servers had all disappeared into the room out the back, and Finlay spotted the coffee tray set out near the door to that room.

"I'll get us both a cup," he said, jumping out of his chair. "You escort your guests through, and I'll be there in a moment."

Standing near the coffee pot, Finlay must have broken the world record for the longest time it took to make two cups of black coffee. The door to the back room was closed, but Finlay had very sharp hearing.

It would seem the mystery person didn't talk a lot, but then Finlay heard the scrape of a chair, and the voice spoke again in response to something one of the other men had said. The man sounded amused, but that moment was quickly lost as the door opened and the staff came out, heading for the tables.

Picking up the cups quickly, Finlay walked past just as the door was swinging closed and caught the glimpse of a slender back and a long silver plait hanging down against a black shirt before the door closed fully. Definitely not one of the servers.

I need to know who you are. Finlay didn't know why exactly, but as he went through to the meeting with his brother and his guests, he was already forming excuses he could make to his brother on why he had to leave the meeting again. And fast. It wasn't going to take forever for the efficient staff to clear the room and head for home, and one could assume the mystery man, whoever he was, would be leaving with them.

Chapter Five

"Hey, Wyatt, what's going on?" Senan glanced up to notice that Wyatt was still loitering around the door that the others had left at least a few moments before. "Did you forget something, or did you want to have a word?"

Wyatt stood nervously twisting his hands in front of him. "I just thought I should check in before heading out. I'm a bit worried I didn't do a very good job this evening."

Senan frowned. "What makes you say that?" He dropped the dishcloth he'd been cleaning up with and stripped off his rubber gloves. His hands felt clammy from being encased in the rubber for so long, and Senan rinsed them under the tap and then reached for a dry cloth.

"It was a good night as far as I could tell," he said. "There were no plates broken, nobody got any food spilled on them. From what I understand there were absolutely no complaints, and definitely nothing about you specifically. What made you think that you'd done something wrong? You've been doing really well."

Wyatt had joined the team about three months before. He was young, no more than nineteen or twenty most likely. He was tall, but had a slender build, which might have been because he had trouble sitting still, standing still, or being still for any reason. He was really intelligent and studying computer science, at least that's what Senan had been told.

While Senan could work his way around a computer if he had to, he wasn't likely to know how to pull one apart or to be able to fix it if something went wrong. Wyatt had laughed when Senan had mentioned his lack of expertise, claiming that when he got his degree he'd be the person who Senan would be getting in touch with to fix the computer errors he'd made.

Wyatt did seem to have a problem with interacting with others at times, as if he wasn't sure how he was meant to act. He got along well with everyone at the catering company, but he did struggle occasionally with guests.

"Let's have a seat for a moment," Senan said, glad to take the weight off his feet. He dearly wanted to go home, but as he had seniority over Wyatt, he knew if he could help him, the way Gabby had helped Senan when he first started his job, then Senan would do it. It was a way of paying things forward.

"There was this guy, one of the guests." Wyatt sat down, but again the movements were jerky and quick, as though he wasn't sure what to do with his limbs. "This is going to sound weird, but he kept looking at me."

Senan's first instinct was to brush it off. It wasn't against the law for anybody to look at another person even if they didn't welcome the glances. But he stopped himself.

Wyatt wasn't a whiner. Yes, he got distracted easily. Yes, he sometimes had to be prodded to be reminded to stay focused. But he had a brilliant mind, and he wasn't the type to make a complaint about nothing. He worked hard. He told Senan that his goal was to complete his studies and not have any student debt. So it wasn't as though he was a flake.

Then there was the fact that the event had been specifically paranormal - host and guests. Wyatt, like everyone else Senan worked with was human. But Senan knew more than anybody how disconcerting some paranormals could be, especially Alpha types.

"Is this your first paranormal-only event?" he asked quietly.

Despite paranormal's having been out for well over a hundred years, it was very rare to have paranormal-only events. The events Senan and his colleagues usually attended had a mix of all species that were more interest, business, or hobby specific, like the gardening group he'd worked at during lunch. "Don't you have a lot of experience with shifters and vampires and the like?"

"About the same as anyone else, I suppose. I'm not a hater," Wyatt added quickly in case Senan thought he might be. "About half of my class are shifters of some type, and I get along fine with them. There was just something about this guy. He seemed so intense. I kept thinking that he was watching and waiting to jump on me for doing something wrong. That was the only reason I mentioned it. I'm not trying to cause any trouble for him or anyone else."

"Hey, that's okay. I do know that. And the shifter watching you could've been doing that for any number of reasons," Senan said. He had no idea why anybody would single out Wyatt.

It wasn't that the man wasn't goodlooking, because he was in a geeky way.

But it would be unusual for a person as young as Wyatt to attract a paranormal's interest unless they were mates. Senan already knew that if Wyatt had been that intense man's mate, he wouldn't be loitering in the kitchen worrying about his job. He'd already have been swept off to do goodness knows what.

"The thing you need to remember about paranormals," Senan said, keeping his voice low, even though the guests had gone into their other room for their meeting, "is that they do get fixated on rather strange things. It might have been the way you wore your hair, or maybe the way you smiled or moved. It could be that this paranormal wasn't looking at you specifically at all, but you just happened to be in his line of vision, and he was intent on one of the other guests. Is that possible, do you think?"

"I don't know. I suppose it could be." Wyatt shrugged. "I just... they were all very intense, you know, and I mean any other time, at any other event, you know, if somebody had done that, I would have just turned around and asked them if they had wanted something. But I couldn't do that here because of all those rules we had to follow. It felt strange and a bit weird."

"I think you'll find the rules were put in place by a very detailed Alpha who was determined that his guests have an enjoyable evening without any distractions. If you think about it, how hard it might be for a wolf shifter, or a bear, for example to try and enjoy the delicious-smelling steak Maisie and her team prepared, but they couldn't smell it because you'd decided to wear cologne for the evening.

"It's not up to us as servers and dishwashers to question a host's requirements for a specific event. What I do know is that in the two years I've worked for Jeffrey, this is probably only the third specifically paranormal event he's catered for. You know yourself in most events we're encouraged to be friendly, and introduce ourselves to our tables. Maybe it was you not doing that this time that just made the whole event seem weird from the start."

"It could be that, too." Wyatt nodded.

"Be sure to tell Gabby about it next time you see her." Senan smiled, as Wyatt looked up, his eyebrows raised. "She was horrified she wasn't even picked to attend. She got most indignant about servers being expected to blend into the wallpaper."

"It felt like that, yeah," and clearly because Senan was normalizing what Wyatt had experienced, Wyatt was feeling better about it. "I was just... I was so self-conscious and worried I would do something wrong and the more I worried about it, the more likely I was going to trip over my shoe or embarrass myself."

"You stayed on your feet. You didn't drop anything. You did really well, and I know Jeffrey's pleased with you or he wouldn't have put you on this event. Remember you got in when Gabby didn't. Ask her about that next time you see her as well if you enjoy having your ears scorched."

Wyatt laughed. The man really was an open book, and that was nice to see, even if it made Senan feel jaded. "Look," Senan added. "It's Friday night. You've done your job. I don't know whether you're going to be like Aisha and at home studying tonight, or if you're going to go and have a drink with your friends."

"Drinking tonight, studying over the weekend," Wyatt said. "Brennan and Alex are waiting for me in the parking lot. I told them I needed to talk to you because, you know, I really do need this job. My family couldn't afford to send me to college. I'm doing this on my own, so working is really important to me."

Senan didn't have a clue what that was like. It wasn't as though he'd ever gone to college. But he nodded as if he understood. A strong work ethic was always something he appreciated.

"Honestly, don't worry about it. Go and have a drink with the others. Put that man, whoever he was, out of your mind. The one thing you can count on with anyone rich enough to hire Jeffrey's company is that they are always the quickest to make a complaint if they have any. Tonight went off without a hitch, so go and enjoy your weekend. Paranormals are like anyone else in a way, and they all have their quirks. I'm sure you have nothing to worry about."

"Phew, thanks Senan. I appreciate it. You look absolutely dead on your feet as well. Are you going out tonight or are you heading home?"

"I'm heading home, definitely home," Senan said. "I've had enough of peopling and dishes to last me a lifetime. I'm going to order takeout that comes in boxes, so I don't have to wash my own dishes, and I'm just going to sprawl on my couch and watch ridiculous movies on television."

"Sounds like fun." Wyatt jumped up from his seat and headed for the door. "Enjoy yourself, Senan, and thanks."

He disappeared, and Senan let out a long sigh as he stood up a lot slower. *I feel like an old man,* he thought feeling the ache in his bones. He knew what it was. He was overdoing his magic usage, but Senan still had a job to do which meant he had to hang on just a short while longer.

Speaking of work... Senan grabbed hold of the clipboard, ticking off the last of the jobs, so he could take the paperwork into the office on Monday. Putting that down, he picked up a cloth, giving one last wipe over the surfaces and then collected the dirty cloths and put them in the hamper provided by the convention center. He was leaning against the sink, reading through the checklist one last time when he heard an unfamiliar voice.

"Excuse me. Can you tell me where I can find some bottled water?"

Senan immediately spun around so he was facing the wall, his magic blaring it's distress. *There's a wolf shifter in the room.*

"Excuse me? Did you hear me? I'm just looking for water."

He's not here to see me, he's not here to see me. I'm just a staff member. Pull yourself together. "I believe there's a cooler farther down the hallway, on the way to the lobby,"

Senan said, gripping onto the side of the sink to keep him upright.

"Thank you. By the way, I don't think we were introduced. I didn't notice you with the serving staff when we arrived."

"I wasn't rostered on the server side of things this evening. Somebody has to take care of the dishes. If that's all, I need to head out now."

Senan had no idea how he'd managed to keep his voice so calm, but he didn't dare turn around. It was an instinct, as if the moment the man, whoever it was, saw his face, he would *know*. Senan couldn't name the fear, but he knew there was one there. *Just go. I can't get out of the door if you're standing in front of it.*

But the man behind him was persistent. What was worse, he was sniffing the air. Senan could hear him. "Shit, that's unusual. Why can't I smell you? Why don't you smell of anything?"

"I'm sure I do." Senan waved the clipboard in the air as if he could shoo the man away. He could hear the shifter getting closer. "It really doesn't matter if I smell of anything or not," he added quickly. "You've had your meal. There's water in the cooler down the hall. If you'll excuse me, it's time for me to go home. Good night." *Piss off!*

"Humor me, if you don't mind. I need you to turn around. I want to see your face."

I don't fucking think so. But even as he thought that Senan felt a rush of anger, along with a push from his magic to be set free. No wolf shifter had the right to accost him just because he'd wandered into a room and was being nosy.

The wolf shifter wasn't even supposed to be in a prep area reserved for staff. Senan had done his job, a job that he got paid for, and nothing in his job description said he had to spend any time with a wolf shifter who he didn't know and had no intention of getting to know – no matter what his magic thought.

Swinging around, the clipboard still in one hand, Senan got his first look at his intruder, and his eyes widened. *It's just not possible.* "You! What are you doing here?"

He got a frown and a slight head tilt. "I definitely don't think we've met before. I sure would've remembered someone who looks like you, especially a person with no scent." The wolf shifter did seem genuinely confused.

Narrowing his eyes, Senan looked at the wolf shifter, picking up subtle details like the thickness of the neck, the length and wave of his hair, and the dark eyes. "You're right. Not the you I was thinking of. You're someone similar in looks to a person I have no wish to see. Why are you bothering me?"

"I'm just curious." The wolf shifter had the audacity to look him up and down. "You can call me Felix the Cat. I want to know why a man like you, who clearly has paranormal origins, is hiding among humans, in a prep area, washing dishes, and working for a catering company. Acting as though you're human with limited means when you and I both know you're not."

"It doesn't matter who or what I am, because you and I will never see each other again. Leave. Now. I've had a long day and want to get home."

"Just one more thing..." That was the problem with wolf shifters. They never fucking listened. "Keep your name to yourself if you must, but *what* are you, and who the hell made a mess of your face? Why didn't you heal?"

He reached out as if he wanted to touch Senan's face and Senan snapped as he leaned back. He was exhausted, his magic had been sending alarm bells for the last twenty minutes. He'd worked a full evening terrified of simply being near the largest known predators and not being able to show it. It was almost a relief when that control shattered. Senan's glamour fell away, his wings split his shirt as they unfurled, and his scent suppressor fell to dust.

The wolf shifter took a step back, clearly affected by him, although Senan had no idea why. Barely holding himself together he said, "Look if you must. Look long and hard because this is the last time I will ever be within touching distance of you." He pointed to the mark that was so much more ragged without his human glamour, and grimaced. "Do you have someone in your life or family that looks almost exactly like you? Another Alpha wolf shifter – the heir of the Luna Pack perhaps?"

The wolf shifter's nod was sharp and decisive. The man seemed to be wrestling with himself, his hands fisted by his side and his whole body seemed to be humming with tension. "I'm a twin. My older brother, Morgan was the host of this evening's event. He's the Alpha of the Luna Pack, though, not the heir anymore."

Shit, the older Alpha must've died. If Senan had known that he would've quit his job rather than worked the event, no matter what Gabby said. "If you have any more questions about this then, Mr. Felix the Cat in a wolf suit" – Senan tapped his scar – "you can ask your damn twin. I'm ordered to wear this scar for eternity as penance because of the lies he told. That's why I'm here, washing dishes, so I can pay my rent just like everyone else. And no, before you ask, I have nothing left to say to him...or you."

Pulling on the last shreds of his magical reserves, Senon translocated. He was shattered, completely broken. There was no way he could catch an Uber or try to act like a normal human being in the time it would take for him to get home. He didn't even bother to pick up the clipboard that he dropped as his magic came through. Someone at the convention hall could get the papers back to Jeffrey.

He absolutely could not pretend to be someone else for a minute more. He was done!

Chapter Six

MATE! Every atom of Finlay's existence demanded that he shift, sniff, and track the pretty man with the beautiful wings. He held himself back through sheer force of will.

One, he was in a public convention center and the moment he shifted, he'd bring undue and likely negative attention to the Luna Pack. Paranormals were expected to control themselves in public, and every paranormal leader in the state would gossip about him for months if Finlay let go of his wolf.

Two, it wasn't like he could track the man on two feet or four. Finlay wasn't sure if his mate was elf or fae – he was so swamped by how the man's scent made him feel. It wasn't as though he could just scan that scent and match it to the catalog of common scents he held in his brain. His mate disappeared – there one minute and gone the next - and there was no way Finlay could track anyone who did that by conventional means, no matter how much his wolf might want to.

And then there was item three. The reason Finlay's feet were frozen to the floor. His mate, with the wicked scar, seemed to hold his brother, Morgan, as the one responsible. He specifically said Morgan lied about it. *But lied about what?*

It must've been ten minutes, maybe more, before Finlay could force his feet to move enough so he could leave the small prep room. He was loathe to leave the only trace of his mate's scent, slight as it was, but hanging onto a scent wasn't going to help him get answers.

Finlay knew for certain he couldn't see his brother in that moment. Before everything else, Morgan was playing host to eighty-odd guests, so confronting him wasn't an option. Even with his disjointed thoughts, Finlay knew better than to do anything to cause any damage to Morgan's reputation.

But as he walked through the convention lobby, stopping to grab a packet of cigarettes from the vending machine and buying a lighter from the small kiosk next to reception, on his way out the door, Finlay realized the cryptic words his brother mentioned about being cruel might actually have some substance after all. *What could be crueler than lying about an injury he'd caused?*

Lighting a cigarette, Finlay leaned against the hood of the car, staring up at the stars. One of the reasons he was good at what he did was because Finlay had a unique skill that enabled him to pick out pieces of random information and pull them all in together until they formed a cohesive picture. *Although I haven't got a lot of pieces to work with right now.*

A magical being...scarred face...lies...cruelty...an injury caused by Morgan? Finlay wasn't sure about that last part. But he couldn't deny the scar on the magical man's face could definitely have been caused by a claw.

A mark of shame perhaps...penance...working and living as human even though he still has magic...

Finlay's skills were deserting him. He puffed on his cigarette, blowing large plumes of smoke into the night air, before stubbing it out on his boot and putting the butt in his pocket.

It would help if I had the man's name at least. Then I could search the shifter records and see what the case details were. There has to be one. The man basically said he was being punished.

Then Finlay groaned and tapped his head. He didn't need his mate's name to find the case records. He knew his brother's name as well as his own. Pulling his phone from his suit jacket pocket, Finlay typed in a web address very few people knew, accessing the back end of the Shifter Council database.

Adding his brother's name to the search, Finlay frowned as he saw three entries. The first two were typical of all shifters. There was a notification of Morgan's birth and then the formalization of Morgan's position as Alpha of the Luna Pack after their father's death. The third entry was a sealed court case that fell on the year before the second entry. It wasn't a public file and required a security code to open.

And I just happen to have an override code, Finlay thought grimly. Case files were only secured in the most serious of cases, or in situations where the details becoming public could cause an issue to a high-ranking figure. Tapping on the link, Finlay entered his code and lit a second cigarette as he waited for it to load and open.

The details were surprisingly sparse for a locked case. According to the records Morgan, then Alpha-heir of the Luna Pack, had approached a fae later identified by the Fae Court as Prince Senan of Blackstock and asked him if he wanted a friendly drink.

The Prince was apparently so insulted by the offer, he attacked Morgan with magic, causing Morgan to defend himself, resulting in wounds to the fae's face and chest.

A couple of Shifter Council guards happened to be in the same bar, and slapped anti-magic cuffs on the fae, preventing any further damage. *What damage? Morgan's never suffered any physical damage.* Finlay had shifted often enough with the man to know that for a fact. After taking Morgan's testimony, the guards took the fae into custody. There was only one other notation on the file.

After consultation with the Fae Court and Alpha-heir Morgan it was determined the fae would be banished from the fae realm, and he was to wear his scar as penance for the rest of his existence. Alpha-heir Morgan determined he was satisfied with the verdict, and no further investigation was required.

"No further investigation...? What the fuck? Where's the information about why the prince felt insulted in the first place?" Finlay scrolled through the rest of the file.

It was clear from a few clicks that there had been no investigation. No one had taken a statement from Prince Senan, there had been no court case or defense offered by the Fae Court. There was no information about why Prince Senan had attacked Morgan because it appeared no one bothered to ask him.

Morgan claimed it was unprovoked, and his word was believed by the guards who took the prince into custody. Beta wolves, Finlay noticed, and yes that was relevant.

But not to the Shifter Council apparently. There was nothing else. Case closed. No one had appeared to ask for Prince Senan's side of the story at any point in the proceedings. He had been sentenced and punished based on the word of an Alpha-heir wolf shifter, and the two shifter guards who just happened to have anti-magic cuffs on them at the time.

Finlay cleared his phone screen, and put his phone back into his pocket, lighting his third cigarette. He was going to stink of them, and Morgan was bound to complain, but in that moment Finlay did not give a solitary fuck.

Cruel was the word Morgan had used. Lies was the word Prince Senan had used, and on the surface of things, both parties could be believed equally. Shifters could scent a lie a mile away...

Unless the truths the guards were being told by Morgan were only half-

truths, and Prince Senan wasn't allowed to talk at all.

Finlay had seen that happen more than once and as he thought over the brief words he'd exchanged with the prince, he realized his mate didn't even use Morgan's name, only his designation.

My mate wasn't given a chance to face his accuser. Morgan probably found himself another fuck that night, leaving Prince Senan to be locked up, tried, and punished without having a chance to speak up for himself.

Finlay was grinding his teeth, he was so angry, and having to wait for Morgan for what felt like freaking hours didn't help. The packet of cigarettes was half empty by the time Morgan finally left the convention center, waving at Lord Falcon and Gabrielle, the leader of the bear clan south of town, before heading to the car, swinging his keys in his hand as if he didn't have a care in the world.

"Where the fuck did you slope off to?" Morgan said as he got closer. "You left me dealing with the meeting entirely on my own."

"I told you before we left the house, you didn't need me to hold your hand." Finlay snatched the keys out of Morgan's hand. "Get in the car. I'm driving."

"Fuck. Something's clearly crawled up your ass and died." But Morgan went around to the passenger side of the car, and within a minute, they were on the road. Finlay already had a destination in mind, and he pushed the car as fast as it could go in his rush to get there.

Morgan hadn't noticed. He leaned back in his seat, his eyes closed. "Gods, I had such a good night. You were right. I really needed to get out of the pack house for a bit. I was on such a downer before the meal and feel so much better. It's amazing, don't you think? You can mix with like-minded people for a while, and it's a reminder that we're actually independent adults instead of a figurehead everyone around me seems to want to complain to or about all the time.

"Getting dressed up, even simple things like voicing an opinion and actually having it respected. Gabrielle had a couple of really good ideas about limiting the complaints aspect among the pack. No one in his clan complains about anything – they just get on with their lives. Imagine how much easier life would be if the pack was like that."

Finlay grunted. He'd traveled extensively and in his opinion a pack was only as good as the Alpha who looked after them. Not that Morgan was listening.

"Falcon was talking about the bonds between packs, clans, prides, and covens. He was right in what he said about us only really getting together once a year. I'm thinking we could come to a treaty deal with either the vampires or the bear clan. Falcon and Gabrielle both have daughters old enough to form a bond, and if you and I took one each, we'd really increase the standing of the pack."

Snorting, Finlay shook his head as he indicated and turned off the main road, taking a winding road that went up the hills about a thirty-minute run from the pack grounds. "You can forget about including me in any shit like that," he muttered, focusing on the road. "I'm not bonding with anyone."

"Did you forget I am your Alpha?" Morgan chuckled. "If I order it, you have to obey."

"You try forcing me to do something like that and I'll cut my bonds with the Luna Pack permanently. Don't think I won't."

"Gods, you're so fucking moody this evening." Morgan sat up and then frowned as he looked out at the darkness. "Where the fuck are you taking us? Did you take a wrong turn?"

"Nope. We'll be there in a minute."

"We're nowhere near the pack house, or your house, either. Fin, what the hell's going on?"

"We need to have a private chat." Finlay swung into the small parking area he'd been looking for, hitting the brakes and turning off the engine the moment the car had stopped. "So, we're having one. No one will bother us out here." He flicked on the overhead light and glared at his brother who was looking confused for a moment before his face cleared.

"Oh, is this about what I said before we got to the event tonight?" Morgan clicked his fingers. "Just forget I said anything. Honestly, I was feeling dragged down and got depressed and anxious about nothing at all. You were right. I just needed to get my head off my desk for five minutes and talking to people in similar positions to mine was a great way to clear my mind. There's nothing to discuss because I'm fine now."

"We have plenty to talk about." Leaning over, Finlay opened Morgan's car door before straightening up again. "Get out of the car."

"Why?" Morgan didn't move.

"Because when I smash your head in I don't want to get blood on the upholstery."

"But it's my car." Morgan's eyes widened. "Seriously, Fin cut this out. I've got shit to do at home."

Opening his own door, Finlay climbed out and walked around the front of the car, illuminated by the headlights he'd left on. "I had an interesting chat with someone this evening, when I went looking for water."

"Can't have been that interesting. You didn't come back to the meeting, and you've been in a right bloody mood since before I got in the car."

Morgan climbed out of his seat and wandered around to the front of the car, just as Finlay knew he would. "Are you going to tell me what's going on?"

Moving quickly, Finlay grabbed Morgan by the lapels of his jacket, pushing him over the hood of the low-slung car, using his body weight and his forearm across Morgan's neck to keep his brother pinned. "What do you know about the fae known as Prince Senan of Blackstock?" he snarled.

Chapter Seven

Morgan's face went white, and any fight he had in his body completely drained away. "Where did you hear that name?"

"Tell me what you know and talk fast, or I swear I'll walk away, and you'll never see me again." Finlay resisted the urge to reshape the curve of the hood with Morgan's head…just.

"It was nothing. There was a minor incident…a misunderstanding. It happened years ago, before I was Alpha. The case was resolved and closed by the Shifter Council. There's nothing else you need to know."

"You asshole!" Using Morgan's neck for leverage, Finlay pushed himself upright, pacing in the light beams left by the headlights. The temptation to remove his brother's head from his body was raging through him, and Finlay knew the only reason he didn't do it was because he'd be left as the fucking Luna Pack Alpha, and he had no intention of ever holding that position. Doubly so now.

Whirling around, he pointed a finger at his brother who was sitting upright, rubbing his neck. "You will tell me every single detail of that so-called misunderstanding. Every minute fact, regardless of how insignificant you think it was, and you'll do it now. I mean it, Morgan. Don't push me on this. I demand to know."

"Who's been talking about this?" Of course, Morgan would be worried about his own reputation. "That case was supposed to be sealed by the Shifter Council. No one can access it unless they were given permission by the Paranormal Council."

"Who the hell do you think I work for?" Finlay flung up his hands. "What do you think I'm doing when I go away for days or even a week at a time? Landscaping? Putting in someone's new swimming pool? Are you so self-centered you didn't notice the guns and knives I was putting away when you picked me up this evening? I've been a negotiator for the Paranormal Council since I left the pack. I'm the guy who comes after assholes like you."

Morgan actually looked relieved. "Phew. Thanks. I can see why you wanted to keep this chat private now. That means a lot. But why is this case being investigated again? The whole thing was put to bed years ago. Has someone changed their story? Is someone in the fae realm looking into this? Do I need to get a lawyer?"

"You're unbelievable, do you know that?" Finlay wasn't giving his brother a compliment. "How about we start by you telling me how 'being cruel to an innocent' fits in with the case between you and Prince Senan?"

"I should've known you'd throw my words back in my face." Morgan wandered out of the light and leaned against the trunk of a nearby tree, his face obscured by shadows. "I meant what I said. It was a misunderstanding that got out of hand."

"I need details, none of the half-truths you gave two beta Shifter Council guards." Finlay patted his pockets looking for his cigarette pack and lighter. Pulling a cigarette free of the crumpled package, he lit it, shoving the rest of the pack in his pocket again along with the lighter.

"Fuck. Better you know than anyone else." Morgan sniffed. "As far as I'm concerned it was a genuine misunderstanding. I was in the Royal Oak, having a few drinks. When I went up to get another beer, I saw a fae sitting by himself, and just wanted to be friendly."

"I've had experience with your being friendly, remember?" Finlay did. "That's why we almost came to blows when we double dated that last time. You have the seduction skills of a rampaging bull in a china shop and usually cause the same amount of damage."

"You can shut your mouth. A lot of people appreciate a dominating Alpha – a lot of them crave it. Did you want to hear the details or not?"

Of course, Morgan would get defensive. There was a good chance he was still using his "hey, you look good enough to fuck," which was what constituted his only pickup line. "I asked him if he wanted a drink. He said no."

Finlay nodded.

"I sniffed him." Morgan stared up at the night sky. "It was weird. He had the most unusual scent – like he smelled of magic and some kind of floral scent, but it was also as if he reminded me of home and pack. I knew he wasn't my mate, nothing drastic like that. But the scent was intriguing, and I was lonely and horny. Face it, any hole works in the dark."

That's my mate you're talking about. Clenching his teeth together, Finlay nodded again. His brother was cruising for a bruising, heading for Smash Town in the fast lane. He forced himself to unclench his fist, taking another puff of his cigarette.

"I figured he just needed a spot of sweet talk, so I took the stool next to him, sitting close enough so I couldn't be ignored, but not on his lap, you know."

"We're a long way from you invading his personal space, to him ending up with permanent scars."

"Not really." Morgan shrugged. "I was talking to him, trying to engage him in conversation. He kept saying he wasn't interested, but he had to be, right? He had to be interested, otherwise, he would've just left his seat and gone and sat somewhere else."

"I can't believe you just said that." Finlay took a step closer and then stopped himself. If they started fighting, Finlay might never get the whole story. "Maybe Prince Senan was simply staying in the chair he was in before you came along and decided he wasn't going to get run off by an arrogant wolf shifter. Or, maybe he didn't know a lot about shifters and worried if he did get up and leave, he'd trigger your hunting instinct, and you'd chase him down and start fucking humping him. Did you ever think about that?"

"Nah, that can't be true, can it?"

My brother has the brains of a gnat. "He said no to you. The only decent response from you at that point was to apologize, or if you couldn't manage that, then you should've just got up and left the man alone." Finlay was shouting, and he pulled himself in with difficulty. "How did he end up with your claws in his face? You said in the report that he attacked you with his magic."

There it is. Finlay saw Morgan shift his weight from one foot to the other, shoving his hands in his pants pockets. Finlay had seen Morgan do that a hundred times when their father used to pull them into his office for *misunderstandings*. "That's where there might have been a bit of a stretch to the story. I put my hand on his knee, still being friendly and then when he ignored it, I moved my hand up his thigh... He zinged the back of my hand."

Finlay squeezed his eyes tight, trying to blank out the mental image of the scene Morgan was describing. "What the hell is a zing? Is that like a zap? A little twinge of electricity on your skin, probably used as a warning to stop your hand from going anywhere near his cock? That kind of zing?"

"Well, yes," Morgan blustered. "But it stung, and it was a shock. He wasn't dealing with a regular shifter, I was Alpha-heir at the time. It annoyed me, and I lashed out, not even realizing because of the zing, my claws were out. He was bleeding, his top torn and everything else. I was horrified by what I'd done. I was trying to work out if I should apologize or get him medical treatment when the shifter guards were there, putting him in cuffs and dragging him away. There was nothing else I could do at that point."

Huffing out a long breath, Finlay said, "So, you never told the shifter guards you'd been attacked? They made that bit up?"

"No, I did say that. But what would you do if two guards were suddenly in your space, dangling cuffs and looking like they were going to arrest me for goodness knows what? Dad would've been horrified, and I was terrified he'd find out. So I just yelled, 'he attacked me with magic,' and yeah, they took him away. I don't even know what happened to him."

"Don't you dare start bullshitting me now," Finlay snarled. He stubbed out his cigarette and stuck that in his pocket. It was getting full. "According to the case notes, Prince Senan of Blackstock was banished from the fae realm and ordered to wear his scar as penance for what he'd done for the rest of his life. The case notes specifically state that you personally agreed to that punishment."

"Well, fine, but what else did you expect me to do?" Morgan huffed. "If I told them I overreacted, I'd have looked like a fool. I couldn't look bad in front of the Shifter Council. They would've told Dad and I could've lost my position as heir. So, I just agreed and figured the fae would make the best of it. They usually do. You know, I have to say, it's a relief to be able to talk about it, to be honest."

Finlay ran his hands through his hair. He'd been running on fumes before the damn dinner event, and it was only the need to do right by his mate that was keeping him upright. "So let me just make sure I've got all the details right, do you mind?"

"I don't care. I feel so much better now it's out in the open."

"I'm glad for you." Finlay wasn't. "To hear you tell it, you approached a man at a bar. He said he didn't want a drink when asked. You ignored his clear cue to be left alone and encroached on his personal space. He told you he wasn't interested. Then you put a hand on his leg, and when he ignored that, you moved your hand up his leg, I assume you planned to cup his dick and see what he was packing?"

"I thought it was a friendly thing to do, you know. Let him know I would take care of his needs while he was letting me fuck him."

"How fucking big of you." Finlay exploded. "Why the hell didn't you just leave him alone?"

"I thought he was just playing hard to get. People do that, you know."

"No they fucking don't." Finlay lunged, his fists flying before he landed on Morgan's body. They both fell to the ground. "No means fucking no, asshole," he grunted, pummeling his brother's face and chest as he straddled him. "He said no. Not once. Not twice. A dozen times he said no. And you fucking ignored him."

"Fin! Fin! What the fuck man, that hurts." Morgan tried to evade his fists, but while he'd been playing with spreadsheets, Finlay had been working in the trenches, taking out assholes just like his brother. "I don't understand. The case was four years ago. It was a misunderstanding, no one else needs to know about it. Fin, stop it. As your Alpha I'm ordering you."

"You are not my Alpha." Finlay grabbed Morgan by his jacket lapels, lifting his chest off the ground as he snarled. "You will never be my Alpha. I'm breaking my bonds with the Luna Pack."

"What the fuck, Fin, why? It was one little mistake ages ago. I don't even know where Prince Senan is right now."

"I don't know where he is right now, either," Finlay said through bared teeth. "But I know where he was earlier this evening."

The surprise was evident in the white of Morgan's eyes. "You've seen him? Where?"

"He was washing the dishes made dirty by your fancy guests this evening."

"Fuck." Morgan winced and wouldn't meet Finlay's eyes. "That's a step down for him. He used to be part of the Fae Court. But I still don't see why you care. I'm your only brother, he's a random stranger."

"Is he?" Pulling Morgan's head up so their foreheads met, Finlay said quietly, "There was a reason why Prince Senan's scent smelled of home and pack when you came across him four years before. It was because he was meant to be family, to be part of the pack."

"I don't get it."

"Prince Senan of Blackstock is my fated mate, and thanks to you being an absolute asshole of the highest order, he won't even talk to me." Finlay shoved his brother's chest back on the ground and stood up. "And from now on, I have no intention of having anything to do with you, either."

"He's your mate? Fin, that's great news." Morgan scrambled to get up. "You can bring him into the family...we can chat about it...I'll even apologize...we can look after him. Finlay, where are you going? Fin, come back!"

Finlay flipped his brother off behind his back and headed back down the road on foot. The moment he was out of sight of the car and his brother, he shifted, making sure to keep his phone securely in his jacket which he picked up in his jaws. His wolf wanted a run, and they'd cover the ground to home a lot quicker that way.

After that, he'd get a few hours' nap, and then it was time to start tracking the elusive Prince Senan. Finlay just had to hope that the mating pull for fae worked the same as it did for shifters. Although, that was a double-edged sword as well. If he didn't find the prince soon, they could both be in the shit.

Chapter Eight

Senan was wrecked. He knew that he had overdone his magic usage on the Friday night event. Somehow he'd managed to maintain his magical glamour for more than twelve hours without a break, and that was without the scent suppression magic he'd been using while he was at the second event.

He had been working during that time as well, which had its own physical toll. And then, with the confrontation with the wolf shifter at the end of the night, he expected to at least feel tired over the weekend.

But it was now Monday afternoon, and Senan couldn't muster up the energy to produce enough glamour to even get him into work, let alone act like his life was normal.

For the first time in his two years employment, Senan called in sick. He hated lying to anyone – his wearing a glamor every day was enough of a lie in itself - but his voice as he made the call sounded croaky and out of sorts even for him. Betty, who had taken the message for Jeffrey, assured him that no, he was doing the right thing in staying home and that there were plenty of colds and flus going around. "You've been working a lot lately, so you were bound to come into contact with germs."

She recommended that he have hot lemon and honey drinks, and to make sure he got plenty of sleep. Senan had tears in his eyes as he thanked her and got off the phone. That simple act of kindness reminded Senan how lucky he was with the non-paras in his life.

If only I did have the flu or a cold. Paranormals didn't get sick in the same way non-paras did, and Senan knew he was suffering from more than just a virus. One could hope that a flu or virus might eventually pass through the body, but Senan was starting to think he might be permanently afflicted with whatever it was that was making him feel so exhausted.

His brain wasn't doing him any favors either. Senan didn't understand why he couldn't stop thinking about the mysterious wolf shifter from Friday night. The man admitted he was a twin to the man who had wrecked his face and chest and, more than the physical act, had wrecked his life. That first wolf shifter had no thought, caring, or respect for him, who he was, or his right to exist in his own space.

No, on that fateful night, that first wolf shifter had just decided that, for some reason, Senan didn't have the right to say no, didn't have the right to just enjoy a quiet drink on his own, didn't have the right to just be alone in a public space.

Gods, Senan missed those days when he genuinely enjoyed listening in on the conversations around him in a random bar, feeling as though he was being sociable without being part of a conversation. He learned so much about life from the snippets of chat he heard around him, and for Senan that was fascinating.

Until a wolf shifter with delusions about his own sense of self-importance, wrecked everything for him in the space of less than thirty minutes.

After the shock of being arrested, not even being allowed to talk, and then being let go after being slammed with conditions that totally changed his life, Senan believed he had done a really good job of keeping himself together. He put the wolf out of his mind as best he could and turned his whole life around.

For one thing, he didn't let anyone know he was a fae, or even paranormal. He wore a glamour every time he left the house. Part of that was pride. Yes, Senan hated the way his skin puckered and pulled around his scars down his face and across the left side of his chest. But it wasn't as though he went out topless. He could've used makeup to lessen the impact of the scars he had in his natural form, although it would be impossible to cover them completely.

But for Senan the glamour was also protection. He doubted any of his human friends would've cared if he'd met them au-natural so to speak. They might have been shocked, and perhaps asked him why he'd felt the need to lie about who he was, but paranormals were another issue entirely. They didn't see scars the same way as non-paras did, and personally, Senan saved himself a lot of questions and grief, just by wearing his glamour every time he went outside.

Aside from that, Senan used his magic as little as possible, mostly because he only had so much supply and most of that went into maintaining the glamour he used. There was a common public misconception people seemed to have about magic users, that they could just draw on the energies from the earth and sky and have an unlimited tap of power at their disposal.

But that wasn't the case for fae. Fae had a finite store of magic, and it needed to recharge like a battery. Thanks to the culmination of events that happened on Friday night, Senan's battery hadn't just run out of juice, it was as though it had completely exploded.

He didn't dare leave the house. He called in an order for groceries, just a few bits and pieces, so he could at least survive, but he didn't even greet the delivery driver at the door like he normally did. Senan waited until the man had been and gone, and then checked the small street where he lived, peeking out the door to make sure nobody could see him as he quickly whipped his bags and boxes inside. Just doing that wore him out and it took more than an hour to put his small haul away.

Senan was drained - completely and absolutely drained. And while he knew his magic was rejuvenating in its own way, it was more that he felt as if his soul was missing something. Senan couldn't think of any way to describe the incredible sadness that had him crying over a commercial for puppy food. Or the complete lack of motivation to do anything beyond remembering to shower and change his underwear and sweatpants.

As Saturday morphed into Sunday, the soul ache increased. For some reason Senan's magic seemed to think he needed to find the wolf shifter he saw for a brief five minutes on Friday night. Senan was totally confused by that. Why on earth would his magic be so supportive or encouraging - and indeed it was the only thing his magic had any motivation for - in finding that damn man. Finding another wolf shifter who'd pushed himself into Senan's space and refused to listen to him.

In the meantime, snippets of the night he'd gotten his scars kept infecting his dreams. Random memories such as how he recoiled at the smell of his own blood which was all he'd been able to smell for three whole days because his prison guards wouldn't let him wash.

How he'd clung to the tatters of his torn shirt, as if trying to cling onto any shred of decency left in a world that didn't have any, frustration and despair increasing in equal measures as the council guards talked over him, never letting him explain any of his side at all.

And the pain battling with the sheer horror of how badly his life had changed with just one encounter.

But Senan survived, he put his life back together, working hard and keeping a low profile. Until wolf number two came along and showed him how fragile that illusion of normality was.

He felt as if he was being attacked all over again in his sleep. He couldn't go to bed because if he did, his wings kept getting in the way and Senan didn't have the energy to pull them back in. His wings clearly felt that they were necessary as some kind of attraction tool, working with his magic, pushing Senan to find the missing wolf shifter.

Senan was so tired he just sprawled out on his couch, lying on his front so his wings could flutter all they liked, idly watching rubbish on the television screen with no idea of what was on or what he was seeing. His mind just kept going back to two wolf shifter infested nights. If he wasn't thinking about one of the damn wolves, he was thinking about the other one.

Neither one of them are doing me any favors, he thought as he reached for the television remote. *I really need to be able to put all this behind me,* and yet it was as though that part of his brain was completely fucked. He couldn't stop thinking about the night his life was ruined, and if he wasn't thinking about that, Senan was thinking about the wolf shifter who had intruded on him at the event.

It was quite strange in a way, because if the first event hadn't happened, then Senan might have found the second wolf shifter attractive. Yes, the two men looked very similar, but their attitudes were totally different. Senan liked somebody with a bit of brawn. He appreciated men who had that look of someone who could handle themselves in a fight.

The man spoke with a hint of humor as well. "You can call me Felix the Cat," like he was sharing a joke with Senan in some way. And yet Senan's life wasn't a joke. It was a fucking travesty.

Laying on the couch on Monday afternoon, Senan stroked over his scar. He had wondered, the way he had a million times before in the previous four years, if he did glamour away the scar completely, would anybody notice or care? Did the Fae Court keep a check on things like that?

Gods, Senan didn't want to think about them, either. Nobody had come to his defense four years before. Nobody had suggested that Senan must have had a reason for what he'd done. No, no, they had bowed down to the Shifter Council and distanced themselves from him. And Senan knew why - he knew why they didn't rush to his defense or help him in any way.

It was because the assault had happened on Earth. Fae preferred their own realm, a realm that Senan had now been banished from. They saw the attack on Senan as a reason why they should stay on their own realm.

And then there was the little matter of the scars on Senan's face that would've horrified his ex-friends and family because they were ugly.

Senan knew that for a fact. He was just a regular fae, despite his prince title – something he'd gained purely from the circumstances of his birth. But he'd never been one of the truly beautiful ones – the type of fae others looked up to. And maybe that was why it was so easy for the Fae Court to throw him away.

That had hurt so badly back all those years ago. It had stung him hard that nobody - not his parents, nor his sister, nor anybody he'd known on the fae realm, had bothered to ask the Shifter Council to move the case to the Paranormal Court where his side of the story could be heard.

There was no legal advice offered. No one had tried to sue the Shifter Court for keeping him in anti-magic cuffs that completely cut off his ability to heal from the wounds. No one was there in Senan's circle insisting that somebody question the Alpha who had physically hurt him, about what actually happened before Senan was attacked.

I didn't do anything but get him to move his hand. And that was the thing that hit Senan harder than anything else. Being punished the way he had been, it was easy for him to believe that he didn't have the right to his personal space, that he didn't have the right to sit in a chair in a public space and be left alone. He thought he'd had those rights, but clearly, the Shifter Council thought differently, and so did the Fae Court.

Senan had always been the quiet one, even when he lived on the fae realm. It meant a lot to him to be able to observe all types of persons interact with each other without ever feeling he needed to be part of the action himself.

Friday night, after table service was done and before he got accosted by a wolf shifter, was an example of that. Senan was friends with the people he worked with, but he never dominated the conversation. He loved listening to them chatter among themselves in his vicinity.

And now I can't even do that. Senan knew there was no point in even trying to go back to work until his magic stabilized. But with the overwhelming fatigue that was dragging on his limbs making him feel so weak, he wondered if that would ever happen again.

It wasn't that he was hurting for money. While he might have told the wolf shifter he'd met on Friday that he was working to pay the rent - and that was true to a point because his wages were paid into the same account the rent came out of - he wasn't without means. He could *not* work. But Senan had always believed he should do something with his days, and non-paras worked for social and financial benefits. It's what people did, and the fae did not.

Maybe I was washing dishes as another form of penance, he thought. *Maybe I'm punishing myself for a crime I didn't even commit. Perhaps I need to rethink my whole life here on Earth*, although it wasn't like Senan had any other option, like living on a different realm anymore.

He could have moved away from the state, the scene of where the incident happened. The Shifter Council didn't tell him he couldn't move, or restrict where he lived in any way. But there was a spark of tenacity in Senan as well. In his head he felt that it was enough that the wolf shifter had taken away his looks, his right to be on the fae realm, his position on the Fae Court and his chance of ever being viewed as "normal" again, so why should he lose his house as well?

So Senan had stayed, and eventually, he'd found himself a job. That had taken two years for him to get the hang of being interviewed and having a resume. But once he had the job, he'd enjoyed the work. He'd even made a few friends. Living as a human in a lot of ways was so much easier than trying to keep up the superficial pretense of "life is always wonderful" which the fae seemed to insist on.

When he was working with non-paras he learned about their daily struggles, about Aisha's studying and her string of boyfriends – none of whom lasted very long. Brennan was a ladies man who would be happy on Fridays and usually despondent by Monday morning because he'd done something silly, and the lady had left him. There was Wyatt's discomfort and anxieties that his friends would gently tease him about, but they were so supportive of him as a group as well.

Senan adored Gabby, who just took him in and declared him a friend from day one, never caring who Senan might have been aside from the way he presented himself on the job. She was genuinely a good person who just liked him, and for Senan, that was a true gift. *She would never back down or run away from a wolf shifter,* he thought with a grin.

So caught up in the endless loop of his mind, it took a moment for Senan to realize somebody was banging really loudly on his front door. His heart jumped to his throat – what if it was one of the wolf shifters? It didn't matter which one. Senan wasn't ready to face either of them.

His shoulders sagged in relief as he heard Gabby yelling through the door. "You'd better open this door, Senan. Jeffrey told me you're sick and you're never sick. Let me in, or I'm going to call the police to do a welfare check on you."

Groaning, Senan rolled off the couch, trying to muster enough magic to at least put his wings away. But nothing was working. As the pounding got louder, Senan resigned himself to the fact he was going to lose his friend as well. *One look at me and she'll know I've lied to her from day one.*

Stumbling over to the door, he unlocked it and opened it, letting Gabby push her way inside as he staggered his way back to the couch, plonking his butt down and burying his face in his hands.

"Oh, my gods, Senan, what happened to you?" Gabby sounded genuinely worried. Looking up Senan could see that concern on her face. She was wearing one of her most colorful outfits - a bright blue Hawaiian shirt of some kind that fell over her ample frame and knee-length bright yellow bike shorts. On her feet, she had her favorite rainbow crocs, festooned with dozens of little dangles that people seemed to enjoy decorating their footwear with. In other words, she looked like typical after-work Gabby.

"What do you mean what happened? Can't you see? Don't you see?" Senan flicked his wings for emphasis. "I haven't got the magic left to hide me anymore."

To his shock and horror, he burst into tears, and he buried his face in his hands again, half expecting to hear the slam of his front door as Gabby left him to his misery and shame. Seconds later, he found his face cupped in gentle hands that weren't his own.

"How the hell am I meant to hug you with those wings in the way?" Gabby said. "Are they like... like how far down your back do they go? I've never hugged a person with actual wings before, and I want to hug you, you silly fool, because you clearly look like you need one. But those wings keep flapping at me, and I don't want to hurt you."

"Oh, Gabby." Senan leaned forward resting his head on her shoulder, his tears falling even faster in the face of her kindness. "I don't think I can do this anymore. I can't hide who I am anymore, and I'm scared."

Chapter Nine

"You're not angry at me?" The tears had been shed, and the entire story from wolf one to wolf two had been told in halting sentences. Gabby made it so easy for Senan to spill it all, listening the way she did. Now, wrung out emotionally, and cradling the mug of tea Gabby had made for them both, Senan needed the reassurance that Gabby's friendship hadn't changed.

Leaning back against the couch, Gabby shook her head, and then she pointed at his wings, which were still flapping about the way they did. "I've got nothing to be angry about. I can see why hiding your wings at work makes perfect sense. If you think about some of the table layouts where we're expected to serve, I mean, half the time I can't get my generous booty into those spaces, so I can see those wings would be a real hassle. And the shirts – wearing those drab shirts Jeffrey insists on.

Has he got an option for those with wings? I don't think so."

"I never asked. Jeffrey doesn't know about this." Senan flicked a hand at his fae state. "I'm still the same person inside. What I look like might change for work, but I'm still me."

"Sort of like a rather elaborate Halloween costume." Gabby laughed. "No wonder you never wanted to dress up for the company parties."

"You tried to make me wear a wolf shifter costume," Senan reminded his friend, although he felt so much better knowing Gabby didn't hate him even after learning his secret.

"Yes, that business with the shifters is a concern. I understand why you never wanted to work a para event now." Frowning, Gabby tapped her nails on the mug she was holding. "This is me, coming from a non-para perspective, and you can shoot me down or tell me it's none of my business, but is there any chance either one of these shifters is your mate? Paras seem to think they're a big deal, for some reason and I've heard that meeting a mate can make them act out of character."

"Meeting a fated mate is a big deal." Senan thought about how to explain one of the central goals of a paranormal's life. "Paranormals have such long life spans. The Fates, those people we believe weave the fabric of life, pair a paranormal with another person to help combat the loneliness that a long life span can cause."

"You mean you're going to have to watch me die one day," Gabby said bluntly.

"Not for decades, I'm sure," Senan said quickly. He had no idea how old Gabby was, but he imagined she was in her late twenties. "But yes, eventually, unless you end up with a paranormal mate, in which case when you're claimed, you'd live as long as they would. But otherwise, yes, when you're old and gray and sitting in your rocking chair complaining about the youth of the day, I won't look any different than I do now."

"Hmm. I hadn't thought about that side of things before." Gabby wrinkled her nose. "That would suck."

"It does." Senan didn't even want to think about it. That was a situation any paranormal with non-para friends had to deal with at some point in their lives. "But with regards to mates, the Fates match us with someone that is supposedly perfect for us in every way. Not someone the same as us, but a person who complements us. I think the reason why it's a big deal for the paranormal community, is that the bond between a mated pair is so intense."

"Heaps of hot sex every day?" Gabby wiggled her eyebrows up and down as she grinned. "That would be fun."

"You would be thinking that." Senan chuckled at her expression. Gabby had a wonderful appetite for all aspects of life. "But yes, seeing as you said it, really intense and amazing sex, *so I've heard*. But that mate would also be protective, always put your needs first, and will always be on your side. They never cheat, they can't lie to you about anything, and you become the most important person in your mate's world. And vice-versa of course."

"Hmm. That saves a lot of messing around I suppose." Gabby sipped from her mug. "But what if you don't like that person these Fates of yours think is perfect for you? What do you do then?"

"I've never heard of that happening." Senan frowned, but he couldn't think of a single case where a mating hadn't worked. It wasn't always easy, but the Fates seemed to be a good judge of character.

"The whole point of fated mates is that even if... like, say I met someone and I didn't like the way they talked to me, or maybe that person doesn't tip the waiting staff at a restaurant. I doubt a person like that could be my mate, because my mate will fit in with the values I already have. They might live a different type of life, but the values would have to be at least similar for a bond to work."

"But what if that person was ugly? Oh, oh" – Gabby pointed her finger at him – "What if they have hairy feet, or worse, a huge hairy wart on the side of their face?"

Senan couldn't stop chuckling at the horror on her face. "Like Paul you mean?" One of Gabby's more disastrous dates. "Mating is far more than what a person looks like – it's about who that person is."

"Yeah, you keep telling yourself that." Gabby snorted. "I'm not lifting my skirts and dropping my panties for anyone who doesn't give me the shivers inside. But anyway, we've gone off track. Could one of those wolves be your mate?"

"The first wolf definitely not." Senan shivered and not in a good way. "His touch disgusted me, and that's not how it's meant to be between mates. The second wolf didn't touch me..." he trailed off.

"Ah, but did you want him to?"

Senan's first instinct was to say no, but that wouldn't be fair to his friend. "I don't know. My magic wants me to go and find him. That's why these darn wings won't fold away the way they're meant to."

Gabby hooked one of her legs underneath herself and leaned forward. "So he could be your mate?"

Running his hand through his hair, Senan said cautiously, "Isn't that a bit of a leap? My magic might just want us to find him so I can tear strips off his brother – really attack him with magic this time."

Snorting, Gabby shook her head as she laughed. "There's no way your wings would be looking all glittery and pretty if you wanted to wage war on someone. You'd be wearing some kind of armor I've seen in a fantasy novel and carrying a spear.

"Besides, you're not the type. You're a definite pacifist. Nope, your wings remind me of... oh, I can't remember what type of bird it is, but when they find someone they want to mate with, they flutter their wings just like you're doing, and do a little dance."

"I am not dancing for a freaking wolf shifter," Senan protested. *Dance with him, maybe...* "Besides, fae don't prance about when they" - he slumped his shoulders - "actually they do. You've never seen a more prancy person than a fae who wants to get laid. They look like freaking peacocks.

"It would've helped if my mating mark had come in, but a fae has to be a hundred and fifty years old before that happens. If I had my mark, and the wolf was my mate, then that mark would be a paw print and that would give me a clue."

"A hundred and fifty?" Gabby almost fell off the couch. "But that's ages for you to wait. You can't be more than twenty, twenty-five years old now."

Senan pressed his lips together as he shook his head quickly at his friend.

"Thirty? Aw, come on Senan. Honestly, you can't be older than that. I won't believe it."

"Okay." Senan forced a grin. "Did you have plans this evening? Or shall I order in some food, and we can watch movies?"

"You can order some food in when you've told me how old you are."

"Thirty and a bit. Did you want chicken, pizza, or sushi?"

"Pizza with everything on it. How much of a bit? Senan tell me."

"Gabby, if I tell you, then you'll start treating me differently." Senan got up from the couch and plucked his phone off the coffee table, opening the food delivery app. "Paras and non-paras have very different ideas about age and aging. What's the saying I've heard you use before? Something like I'm as old as my hair and a bit older than my teeth?" Senan quickly clicked on one of his saved orders on the app, and within ten seconds, the order was placed. "The pizza will be here in half an hour."

"Forty years old? Fifty? Sixty-four?"

Closing his eyes, Senan shook his head as he sighed. *She's not going to give up on this.* "Double the last number and add four more years." Opening his eyes again, he put his phone back on the coffee table and sat back on the couch.

"You're a hundred and thirty-two?" Gabby's voice could really hit the high notes.

Senan nodded. "I'll be a hundred and thirty-three next month. Do you feel better now?" Then he grinned for real this time. "You do realize your crush, Maximus Khan is older than I am, don't you? He's closer to a hundred and fifty."

"You're shitting me." Gabby thumped the cushion beside her. "He's not, is he?"

"Yep, he is. But if it's any consolation shifters have amazing sexual stamina until they're well over five hundred years old." Senan couldn't stop chuckling. "His hair won't even start to go gray until he's at least that."

"You think you know a person and then you find out they've been holding back all the important information like how old Maximus Khan is," Gabby grumbled.

"Just imagine how experienced he would be." Reaching over Senan patted Gabby's knee. "We'll watch another one of his movies tonight, and I promise, your dashing Maximus will still look as young and handsome as he always has."

"What about your wolf shifter?" Gabby gave him the side-eye. "Do you think you're younger or older than him?"

"I know I'm older," Senan admitted. "Magic has some uses. But it will probably only be about forty or fifty years or so. That's what I mean. Paranormals don't worry about age. Once someone becomes an adult, and that age is different for all species, but once they have reached adulthood then age doesn't matter. I've known some mated couples who have an age gap measured in hundreds of years. But you wouldn't know to look at them, and they don't care."

"Whereas I get messages on that dating app I'm on telling me I'm too old and I'm not even thirty." Gabby flung herself back and blew a raspberry at the ceiling, before sitting back up again. "Okay, let's cue up the movie because the food will be here soon. If we get bored drooling over

Maximus's abs, we can come up with a plan to find that wolf shifter of yours. Wouldn't it be exciting if he is your mate?"

If he is, then he'll find me himself, Senan thought but smiling at his friend, he picked up the television remote and handed it over. "You pick something."

Chapter Ten

Finlay frowned at the taxi parked outside the address he'd found for Senan. The driver was doing something on his phone, and the engine was running. As Finlay turned into the walkway to the porch, the driver noticed him and called out. "If you're going in there, can you let Ms. Gabby know that I'm waiting for her? I did toot, but clearly, she couldn't hear me. Honestly, when those two get chatting, they forget they've booked someone to pick them up."

"Will do." Finlay strode up the path, his body thrumming with tension. It had taken him three long days to track down his mate's address. Three days of dodging Morgan's calls and emails pleading for a chance to talk to him – that was setting Finlay's teeth on edge for a start.

Two of those days were spent waiting for the catering company offices to open. Finlay called them first thing Monday morning, only to be told that, no, he couldn't talk to the owner because the man was nursing an injury sustained over the weekend. The receptionist, who introduced herself as Betty, was very nice and equally very firm when she added that the company had a policy that did not allow them to provide contact details of their servers to clients. "Our management would tell you the same thing, sir. I'm sorry, we can't help you."

So there was that. In desperation, Finlay accessed the Paranormal Council database. His bosses would frown on him going through files for personal reasons, but the urge to find his fae was getting stronger by the hour. Unfortunately, Finlay quickly found that the address listed for Prince Senan was the same as it was when he'd been charged for assaulting Morgan.

And didn't I feel like the idiot when I found out the address was still the same and that my mate hadn't moved house? A lot of fruitless searching through files for signs the fae had moved in other words, for no reason at all.

And now it seemed Prince Senan had company – a Ms. Gabby, whoever the hell that was. *In the history of matings, has anyone had the amount of bad luck I have?*

Finlay still didn't know what he could even say to the fae if the man let him into the house. He'd filed papers with the Shifter Council, breaking his ties with the Luna Pack, so hopefully that would help. But he and Senan might have to move simply to stop Morgan from being a fucking nuisance. Somehow Finlay didn't think Senan would be agreeable to something like that.

I have to get him to accept me first, Finlay reminded himself as he tapped on the front door. The house seemed nice enough from the outside. It was small, but it had clearly been looked after. Finlay was struck by the normality of it all. He liked it. *There's nothing typical about this fae, that's for sure.*

"I'm coming," a woman's voice said as the door opened. "Senan, I don't care what you say. When that man takes his shirt off, there is no way anyone could think he's almost a hundred and fifty years old." She suddenly noticed Finlay standing there. "Oops. Hello. Who are you? You're not my driver."

"He told me to tell you he's waiting for you." Finlay pointed back down the footpath at the parked taxicab. "I'm here to see P... Senan."

"O-kay...wolf shifter?"

Finlay nodded. The woman grinned. "Wolf shifter one or two?"

"Er... I'm not sure?" Finlay had no idea what the woman was talking about.

"That's wolf shifter two, Gabby." Senan appeared at the door.

Shirtless, his wings on full display much like when he'd lost control of his magic three nights before. "You'd better go, or Robbie is going to drive off without you."

"Are you going to be all right?" Finlay realized Gabby was worried about her friend.

"I'll be fine." Senan nodded.

"I'll be calling you first thing tomorrow, and you'd better answer, or I'll be coming around." Gabby turned her attention back to Finlay. "Do you know Maximus Khan? How old is he?"

"Maximus?" Finlay had to stop and think for a minute. "Oh, the movie star. I'd imagine he's close to a hundred and fifty. I attended his birthday party a couple of years ago when I was in Orlando, and yeah, I think he was a hundred and forty-five then."

"For the tenth time, I told you age isn't important to shifters," Senan said with a laugh. "Go on. Don't keep Robbie waiting."

"But he knows Maximus Khan," Gabby protested. "I will be talking to you later," she said, poking Finlay's chest as she hurried past. "I'm coming, Robbie. Keep your shirt on. That man knows Maximus Khan." The car door slammed shut as she got in the taxi, and a minute later, the car's headlights could be seen down the road.

This is it. Turning back to the door, Finlay bowed slightly. "Hello, allow me to introduce myself. I'm Finlay..." he hesitated, and then added quickly, "no last name. A recently made lone wolf who works as a negotiator for the Paranormal Council. I believe you and I are mates."

"You're not claiming an affiliation with the Luna Pack?" Senan was gripping the door as if it was holding him up.

"That was last week. The Alpha and I had words about a previous action of his, and I'm now officially a lone wolf with no pack affiliation."

"I'm sorry. I understand that break must've been painful for you." Senan stepped back from the door. "You'd better come in."

Step one, Finlay thought as he crossed through the doorway and Senan closed the door behind him. *Now don't fuck this up.*

"You'll have to excuse the mess," Senan said, picking up the remains of what had clearly been a pizza meal. "Gabby and I had been watching movies and lost track of time. Take a seat. Did you want a coffee?"

"I don't suppose you have any dark beer, do you?" Finlay had been running on coffee for the past three days. "Just water is fine if you don't." He perched on the edge of a single seat, watching in amazement at the fae with brilliant wings cleaning off the trash from his coffee table and taking it over to a recycling bin in the kitchen.

"Dark beer." Senan tapped his chin. "I think I remember what that was like." He clicked his fingers, and two cans from a brand Finlay recognized appeared in his hands. Coming back into the living area, he handed one to Finlay, and then curled his legs under him on the corner of the couch farthest from him.

I can't blame him for that. Finlay inhaled sharply. And then wished he hadn't. Senan's scent was so much more intense in his own living space, and Finlay's body reacted accordingly. "I feel I owe you an apology," he said haltingly. "I got pushy with you at the event on Friday, and I realize that made me no better than my brother. I am sorry for that."

Senan opened his can and took a swig from it, highlighting the beautiful arch of his neck. "I've never understood," he said slowly as his head rightened up again, "how wolf shifters could have such amazing hearing and yet still not master the ability to listen. But apology accepted. I have no grudge with you."

Relief flooded Finlay's body. But he wasn't out of the woods yet. "About my brother…"

Senan held up his hand in a classic stop signal Finlay immediately respected. "Do we have to talk about him?"

"I feel we should." Not that Finlay was sure anything he said was going to make a difference. Morgan had behaved like a brute and an entitled ass and nothing Finlay said was going to change that. "As I said, you and I are mates. I realized that when I spoke to you on Friday. After you left, I waited until my brother's meeting was over and confronted him about it."

"Always respectful of an Alpha's position. The Shifter Council had a similar attitude." Senan's grin wasn't a happy one. It was more like a grimace.

"Yes. No. Yes, okay, you're right." Finlay recognized he was floundering and hurried to explain. "You have to realize that at that point I only had your word that Morgan was a liar, and I had no idea of how you came to that decision. While I was waiting on Morgan to finish his meeting, I used my access to criminal files and read your case notes…"

"Which would've taken all of five minutes," Senan said grimly.

"Three minutes, and you were right. I was horrified on your behalf." Finlay looked down at the can in his hands. "I had seen Morgan act in a similar way before his incident with you and simply refused to go out with him anymore. I just thought he was a lousy date. I never imagined for a second he'd get pushy with a stranger in a bar."

He looked up to see Senan shrugging. "Now you know. Doesn't change anything."

"It could, but I'm genuinely hoping you won't push me to seek justice on your behalf."

Now Senan just looked confused. "I don't understand what you mean."

"I told you when I introduced myself I'm a negotiator with the Paranormal Council. I could insist your case be reopened due to gross negligence on behalf of the Shifter Council and the Fae Court for that matter. I could give testimony on your behalf and share what Morgan told me about that night, and there is a good chance if I did this, that Morgan would be stripped of his position and jailed for life."

Senan's head tilted slightly to one side, his eyes narrowing. "And you don't want to do that because Morgan is your brother?"

"Yes, but not for the reason you might be thinking. I believe you deserve justice, you deserve to have your name cleared and for your banishment to be lifted. But if Morgan is put away for what was very definitely a crime, then..."

Rubbing his hand over the back of his neck, Finlay added, "Up until last Friday I was Alpha-heir of the Luna Pack. Despite my breaking pack ties that same night, there's a good chance the Shifter Council will insist I take over Morgan's position as Alpha if Morgan goes to jail. There's no one else from our family line, nor any other up-and-coming Alphas in the pack that could take over. I really don't want to run that pack – I never did and definitely don't want to now. I truly don't want that life for us."

"Well, shit. That adds a wrinkle to our dilemma that I hadn't seen coming. It's just as well I never thought getting any sense of justice would be a possibility then, isn't it? Good old Morgan gets to continue to live his life without consequence, and as for us..."

Senan didn't finish his sentence. He just lifted his can to his mouth and had another long drink. After a moment's hesitation, Finlay did the same.

"So," Senan said as he leaned forward a few moments later, resting his empty can on the table. "Now we've got that pesky business about your brother out of the way, what can you tell me about you? I guess I should know something about you personally if we're going to do this mating thing. I don't know about you, but I've had a rough three days, it's late at night, and I could do with some sleep. For starters, give me a good reason why I should be sleeping with you instead of alone."

Finlay choked on the dregs of his drink and used his coughing fit as a chance to think of something semi-intelligent to say.

Chapter Eleven

Senan figured he had nothing to lose by putting his cards on the table, or at least being as bluntly honest as Finlay had apparently tried to be. He didn't want to think about Morgan. He didn't want to think about the ramifications of what might happen if Morgan was finally in jail. There was a part of him – a petty side that, like many people, he kept hidden most of the time - that thought longingly of Morgan behind bars, never allowed to be free again.

But the thought that Finlay was or at least had been the Alpha-heir of the same pack was enough to keep his petty side quiet. The last thing Senan would ever do, or ever want to do, was to be living as part of a pack.

In the meantime, Finlay was clearly shocked by his question, or perhaps it was the way he phrased it. Senan had no idea. But Senan had been telling the truth the way he saw it. He was tired. He wasn't going to be able to sit up for hours as they walked through awkward conversations before jumping into bed together. He'd be asleep before the good stuff happened. Although the moment Finlay had walked in the door, Senan's magic had started sizzling and he almost felt like he was ready to let off fireworks the moment he burped. That helped.

But Senan didn't know anything about the serious-looking wolf shifter who was sitting on his chair looking so damned uncomfortable. *I might as well find out something about him because I'm sure as heck we're going to end up in bed together*. He clicked up another can of beer, noticing how effectively his magic was working again – another thing that had improved from the moment Finlay entered his house. *There must be something about this mating business.*

There was also the little matter of Senan thinking sexy thoughts as well.

There was nothing wrong with his eyesight. Finlay was a sexy man – tall, broad, with shaggy blond hair and intense dark eyes. Senan wasn't a virgin. He'd lost that a long time ago. But he still felt cautious. For one thing, Finlay looked a lot like Morgan, and Senan didn't need that reminder. So he was hoping that something Finlay could share with him might show the differences between him and his twin brother.

"I've got to admit this is a bit awkward," Finlay admitted, looking up and catching Senan's eyes. "I've never been in this position, and I worry that something I say might send you running from me again."

Finlay had a lovely chuckle, especially when he was clearly embarrassed. "One thing I've already learned from you is that if you disappear, not even in a puff of smoke, but just cease to be in that space in front of me, I can't follow you. I find that disconcerting."

Senan kept his grin to himself. "Let's make it easy then, shall we? Put bluntly, I feel I should know something about you. I need to see how different you are from your brother." He held Finlay's gaze, making sure the wolf shifter knew he was serious. "This is not going to be easy for me, but I'm trying," he added quietly.

For some reason Finlay gave the impression that Senan had given him a gift – he seemed actually happy by what Senan had said. *Or maybe he's just glad that I haven't rejected the mating out of hand,* Senan thought. That was equally possible.

"What do you do for hobbies?" Senan asked. "You told me you work as a negotiator for the Paranormal Council, and I can only imagine that's very secretive work that I don't need to know anything about. But what do you do when you're not working? What do you do when you're with your friends? Do you even have any friends?"

"I have a few." Finlay chuckled again. "And no, not from the pack – just some of the guys I work with sometimes. Being friends with anyone in the pack wouldn't have been a good idea, even before you and I met. After my parents died, the pack wasn't happy with two Alphas in the pack house, and as I was the younger son, I left and started working for the Paranormal Council instead. I am part of their national task force, so I do travel all over the country. But because of the nature of the work I do, I do have a lot of down time.

"I like to barbecue – I'm considered a mean grill master. I enjoy having drinks with friends. Actually, now I'm thinking about it I'm afraid you'll probably find me quite boring. I don't have a hobby, although I like the idea of perhaps fixing up an old car one day. I'm not really into sports – I'll watch a game to be sociable, but I don't follow any particular team."

The wolf shifter was looking down at his hands. Senan noticed he had very capable-looking hands. "I see an awful lot of bad stuff that goes on, and I work hard not to let that affect me. When I'm home, I just want my life to be normal.

"I like watching TV shows and movies. I keep the garden tidy. Even simple things like vacuuming the house can make me feel good about my day. I know it sounds weird and probably does to someone like you, but that's who I am. I don't have the urge to go crazy and take up skydiving, or travel to exotic locations. After leaving the pack house, all I've ever wanted is to have a home of my own, and I believe that's important enough to be worked for."

Finlay wasn't lying. Senan had already explained to Gabby that mates couldn't lie to each other, and he knew that to be true. "It's not as if I do anything exciting either. If I had any worries going into this, aside from the obvious, it would be that you might have misconceptions about the fae and expect me to act in a way I probably couldn't live up to.

"From what I remember of the fae when I was living on that realm, they were all about appearances. They spent so much time maintaining elaborate lifestyles. But none of it meant anything, if you know what I mean. Everything about the fae life was surface level because they never cared about what a person might be like on the inside. I know that's one of the reasons why they shunned me when this happened." Senan flicked his hand at his face. "A fae prefers it if they never have to confront ugliness – they never want to. Perhaps that's because underneath they can be some of the cruelest people I know. They simply don't care."

Senan felt embarrassed and shrugged. "I've never been like that. I've always been fascinated by people. It's not that I'm overly sociable, but I'm fascinated by how people... how they interact with each other, the things that they say, the way they express their affection, and their connection with each other. It's always been interesting to me."

He bit his tongue. There was no point in mentioning that was something else that Morgan took away from him. Maybe now Finlay was in his life, Senan might have the chance to be able to people-watch again. They might even do it together.

Senan quickly moved on. "You know I work – my job as a server for the Gourmet Company, and before you ask, yes, one of the key reasons I took the job was because I knew it wasn't something a typical fae might do. Serving people, taking orders, doing a job and being paid a wage. I didn't want to be doing something where I was a figurehead or someone who was employed just to look pretty.

"I've made some good friends with the other servers, and if I can ever get my wings to go down again, I imagine that I'll probably want to continue working, at least in a limited capacity." He glanced at Finlay who was watching him so intently it was as if Senan could feel the heat in his gaze. "From what I know about wolf shifters, they prefer to be physically near their mates most of the time. Is claiming me going to make your work a problem?"

A frown crossed Finlay's face. "To be honest, I hadn't thought of it. But I think it's something that we'll have to work on together. I don't get sent out on cases very often, probably once a month, once every six weeks, or something like that. But when I am away, I can be away for anything up to a week. Usually it's only two or three days, but it really does depend on where I'm going and why.

"Cases like chasing rogues for example, can take a lot of time, and in other cases, I could be in a meeting for days investigating concerns of abuse from a leader of a pride, coven, pack, or similar groups. The job isn't easy. And that's one of the reasons why the Paranormal Council likes people like me to have as much downtime as possible. But then I suppose I could get a regular job instead. Do you think your boss is hiring?"

That was such a surprising thing for an Alpha wolf to say Senan laughed. "You're not exactly the sort of person to blend into the background, which is one of the chief things Jeffrey expects from his servers."

"Your friend Gabby doesn't look like someone who blends into the background, either. She looks like a person with an amazing sense of style. If she can do it, I could give it a try," Finlay suggested.

"I'll be sure to let Gabby know what you said about her. That will make her day, and with regards to the job situation, how about we put that idea on hold for a moment?" Senan said, still chuckling. "Super quick. What sorts of movies do you like to watch? What sort of books do you read, if any? Are you on social media or do you think it's a waste of time? What are you *passionate* about?"

Senan's voice caught as he asked the last question. Finlay held his eyes, and it was as if Senan could physically feel the arousal, that need to be closer to him. It was so much more than a person being hot for him, or him for them. The four or five feet between the couch and the chair suddenly felt like an insurmountable separation that his body really couldn't bear. He could see the answering heat in his mate's eyes.

"Can we talk about this later?" Finlay said, as his tone deepened. "I really need to hold you right now."

Senan nodded. As if that was the cue his magic was looking for, Senan's wings melted into his back where they belonged. Which meant, when Finlay crossed the distance between them, Senan could fully enjoy the strong arms that held him firmly, wrapped right around his back. *I've found my home,* Senan realized as he sunk into the embrace.

Chapter Twelve

Finlay didn't realize until he held the trembling fae in his arms that he had spent his life searching for a purpose separate from the pack, separate from his twin. And as he held Senan as close as he dared, he realized with a thump to his heart he'd finally found it.

Somehow two people from totally diverse backgrounds had managed to find each other thanks to the Fates. And while their beginning wasn't as hassle-free as he'd been led to believe a mating should be, Finlay knew in that moment that everything in his life from that moment going forward would be focused on protecting the bubbly man in his arms.

Yes, bubbly. Senan was literally fizzing...bubbling... There was an essence covering his skin that felt like a soft form of electricity that Finlay quickly realized was his mate's magic. As if reading his mind, Senan said, "I think my magic likes you."

"I know the feeling." Finlay closed his eyes a moment savoring the tingle. It was amazingly arousing. Combined with Senan's scent which was the only thing he could smell, and the feel of his mate's body against his, Finlay's cock was waging a revolt against his pants. Everything in Finlay's body was pushing him to give in to his lust – to strip the man of those offending sweatpants and fuck the man until he couldn't remember his own name.

Finlay held back as best he could. Senan agreed to be held, nothing more. He reminded himself that Senan had been treated badly by his kind before, and he needed to take things slow.

Senan wasn't making it easy though. His arms were stronger than Finlay had imagined as they wrapped around Finlay's neck, and his supple body, cradled underneath Finlay's, was tempting him in all manner of ways. Even the way Senan's long hair fell over Finlay's arms was a tease of silk and softness.

"You should kiss me," Senan said quietly. "You look like you might want to."

"Desperately." Holding himself back became all the harder as Finlay tasted his mate's lips for the very first time. He genuinely believed in that moment it was as if time had stopped.

Finlay wasn't prone to poetic phrases, or even using affectionate terms for people he'd been with. Sex was something he did and had done since he learned what his cock was for. But for the first time, Finlay was conflicted. His cock was nudging his zipper screaming, "Pick me," while his lips were taking the time to map out Senan's own lips, his teeth, and tongue, and that was fucking fantastic as well.

Every sensation with Senan felt magnified, so much more magnified than anything before. His cock was determined to break free of his pants, and Finlay was having a hard time keeping himself in check.

He might have had more luck, just focusing on the kissing, if Senan had just held onto him so their mouths could have their moment. But Senan's hands were mapping out Finlay's shoulders, before moving around to his chest, quickly unbuttoning Finlay's shirt to find the skin beneath.

Finlay groaned as soft fingers caressed over him, tweaking his nipple, and then stroking the skin around it, making him jerk and moan. Senan was making it almost impossible not to just fall on his mate's body and start humping him.

"Please tell me I can... Can I...?" Finlay couldn't even finish the question before Senan had his pants undone and a strong hand gripped his cock.

Finlay groaned, thrusting into the fingers, his mouth still busy with Senan's lips. It was awkward, a lot of fumbling, and Finlay really didn't know where to put his hands, so he settled on stripping away Senan's sweatpants, giving him access to the skin on Senan's torso, butt and thighs.

Breaking his lips free so he could explore the skin he'd uncovered, Finlay looked down, his balls ready to unload at just seeing the way Senan's hand barely met around his girth poking out from his undone pants. Letting his eyes roam upward, Finlay came face to chest with the second half of the scar left by his brother. He refused to let the scar bother him. If Senan could forget about it, then so could he. But even as Finlay thought that, he revised his opinion.

My mate has to know I can adore every inch of who he is.

Brushing his lips across the puckered skin, Finlay kept his thoughts of anger and revenge to himself. He wasn't going to make Morgan's life any easier by having him removed from his Alpha position. Morgan could rot in the mess of his own making. Finlay was only concerned about Senan.

"We need to move this along. I ache inside and my magic's ready to set off fireworks." Senan hooked his leg over Finlay's back. "Touch me. Hold me. Claim me."

There's nothing sexier than a person who knows what he wants, especially, when those wants aligned with Finlay's. He refused to be a pump and dump artist, though, taking his time and teasing himself as much as his mate.

He trickled kisses all down Senan's throat. The elegant arch of his neck was one of the first things Finlay had noticed. He kissed along collarbones that stood out in sharp relief from slender shoulders. He took Senan's nipple in his teeth and gently worried it, not quite sure how much pressure to put on, but the way Senan arched into him was simply beautiful.

"Please tell me you have lube." Finlay wasn't going to apologize for turning up and not having any. He'd needed to find Senan because his wolf and soul demanded nothing less. Lube in his pocket would've been presumptuous.

He ran his hand down Senan's side, following the lines leading to the gentle swell of Senan's butt, his fingers grazing his mate's crack. He felt another zing of magic, and seconds later, his clothes were gone.

Senan chuckled, his lips vibrating against Finlay's chest. "I can prep myself," he said, his voice low and husky. "Magic has many uses."

That deserved another kiss. Finlay inhaled Senan's scent, his tongue mapping out Senan's teeth and tongue, his cheeks, and everything in between. Kissing, devouring, holding, tasting, Finlay knew he was acting like a starving man, but he didn't want to stop.

Senan's hand on his cock was still teasing him just enough to keep him on edge, and Finlay wasn't sure he'd last long enough to enter his precious mate, but he was determined to give it a try. With Senan's leg hooked up the way it was, Finlay moved his hips closer, his cock seeking that delicious little hole.

Better check first. His wolf was eager for the claim, but they absolutely could not hurt their mate. Pulling back with his hips, Finlay went in with his hand instead.

"Ah, your magic is a glorious thing," he groaned against Senan's flesh as his finger sunk deep inside Senan's hole.

"Hmm, don't stop now. Did you want me to turn over?"

Finlay shook his head. "No. I want to see you. I want you to see my face. I want you to know who you're going to bind yourself to for eternity."

Senan nodded and then lay back against the corner of the couch resting his arms on the couch back. Finlay lifted Senan's butt with one hand, grabbing his cock and holding it steady with the other.

The angle was definitely awkward, it wasn't going to be very comfortable. But the only thing Finlay was concerned about in that moment was entering his mate's body, and cementing his claim. The rest of it, the vow to protect, the vow to look after his fae were things he would prove he could do over time. Senan would learn he could be trusted, but for now, Finlay was running on instinct and needed to be joined with his mate.

By the time Finlay had managed to get his cock actually inside his mate's body – and that was a toe-curling experience in itself - Senan had his knees up by his ears and was almost bent in half. In the meantime, the frame of the couch was digging into Finlay's knee.

Use your big head for a minute. Pulling back, Finlay brought Senan with him, swinging his legs around so he was sitting on the edge of the couch with his beautiful fae straddling his lap.

"This makes more sense." Senan chuckled. "Way more comfortable."

He rose up on his knees as Finlay got his cock into position once more. This time the slide down his length felt so incredible both Finlay and Senan groaned.

"I hope you know that I didn't assume this would happen," Finlay panted, trying to distract himself from the inevitable orgasm which felt as if it were mere seconds away.

"Silly wolf shifter." Senan groaned again, throwing his head back and exposing his neck. "What else is a person supposed to do when they're claiming each other? Oh, that feels so good."

Righting his head, Senan looked straight into Finlay's eyes. Finlay couldn't see any challenge in the mischief he saw there. Bending down slowly, Senan nibbled up and down Finlay's neck, causing Finlay's gums to itch. Every touch that Senan made sent a direct signal to Finlay's cock, and there was nothing he could do except sit there as Senan rode him with an elegant grace that Finlay had never seen or been a party to before.

It wasn't one of Finlay's smoothest encounters, despite Senan's gracefulness. For one thing, there was barely any room on the couch, and Finlay was worried he was going to fall off the edge, but he kept hold of Senan, keeping his hips steady, reaching up and kissing him where he could as he tried to match Senan's movements.

Senan sped up, and Finlay knew his orgasm was seconds away. The pressure around his cock made him feel as if Senan's body was demanding his spunk and before he realized what had happened, Finlay's fangs dropped, and Senan tilted his neck.

YES! Blood flooded Finlay's mouth as he unloaded his heavy balls into his mate and cemented his claim with a bite to Senan's neck. Senan's hand slapped him on the side of his neck, and then he felt a pinch of pain as if someone had flicked him with a match, but just as quickly, something in his soul clicked and his wolf howled in his head as pleasure flooded his body.

I've been claimed, Finlay thought, as he felt their bond settle into the back of his skull. *And I'm gonna fall off this damn couch for sure if Senan moves.*

Chapter Thirteen

From the way the bedroom was lit up, it was clearly close to lunchtime when Senan woke up. He stretched, realizing with a grin he'd been sleeping on his back – his preferred way to sleep. *My wings stayed tucked away.* Rolling over, he got a good look at the reason for the ache in his butt and the refreshing feeling that came from getting a decent sleep.

In the daylight, it was easier for Senan to see the differences between Finlay and his brother. Finlay was definitely bigger built and better defined. But it was the non-physical differences that touched Senan's soul. As he lay there, thinking about the numerous times Finlay had loved on his body overnight, Senan realized Finlay didn't have to try to be an Alpha – he just was.

An Alpha in the true sense of the word. Senan grinned quietly when he thought of their fumbled claiming. Anyone else would've fucked Senan up against the corner of the couch, not caring about his comfort. But Finlay moved them the moment he perceived Senan might be feeling squished.

It's the caring that makes the difference, he thought, his smile widening as Finlay started to stir, his hand immediately reaching out, clearly looking for him. Alphas were meant to care for their mates and their packs, but again it didn't seem like Finlay had to strive to be caring. It was a part of his nature.

"Did you sleep well?" Finlay's voice was thick with sleep.

"Very, thank you." Senan chuckled. "I was waiting to see if I'm going feel that uncomfortable morning-after sensation. I'm sure you know what I mean."

"Regretfully, I do." Finlay nodded as he rolled flat on his back and stretched out his arms. "I'm waiting…waiting…waiting…nope. I'm not feeling it. You?"

"No, I'm not feeling it either. This mating bond is quite incredible."

"I think it is." Finlay rolled onto his side again, his hand resting on Senan's belly. "I'm sorry but I'm compelled to ask, are we going to be okay?" His hand strayed up, stroking over the scar on Senan's chest. "Can we get past this?"

Senan snorted as he grabbed hold of Finlay's hand and bit the tip of his mate's finger. "If anyone has anything to get over it's *you*. If I held a grudge against you, felt you were in any way responsible for the shit your brother rained down on my life, or believed I couldn't see past the similarities in looks you share with your brother, then you wouldn't be in this bed. You definitely wouldn't have left your cock imprint in my ass, and you wouldn't be wearing my mark on your neck. Perhaps I should be asking you, can *you* get past this?"

"Why did you bite my finger?" Finlay's lips quickly pressed together, and his chest was jerking with his efforts not to laugh.

"I wanted to be sure I had your attention. Experience has taught me that wolf shifters don't listen." Senan poked his tongue at his mate. "Did it work? Did you hear me?"

"Yes, I heard you my beautiful mate, and to answer your question, yes, I can and will get past the shit that is my brother." Finlay leaned over, his lips brushing Senan's chest. "You do realize he's going to pester us for a while, or pester me at least. He thinks it would be a good idea to talk to you."

Senan laughed as he shook his head, thrilled with the casual affection. "I don't owe him another second of my time. What you do with him is up to you. I appreciate you two are family. But he's not welcome at this house, ever. I don't want to see him, ever. And now we've got that out of the way, can you cook, or do we need to go out for brunch? Only my stomach feels my throat's been cut, and I desperately need to use the bathroom."

"I can cook, but let me take you out for a meal. My wolf wants to show you off and that gives me a chance to pick up some clean clothes while we're out." Finlay grinned, which made him look so much younger. "Of course, it would help if I could find the clothes I arrived in last night. Remember? The ones you magicked off my body in your desire to see more of my skin."

"Like my sweatpants aren't laying on the floor somewhere near the couch." But Senan chuckled, too. Finlay probably didn't realize it, but he was really easy to be around. "My magic can multi-task. Your clothes have been cleaned and are folded neatly, along with your boots, on the chair over by the window." He pointed over

Finlay's shoulder. "For a wolf shifter, you're not very observant."

"My eyes just want to feast on you and only you."

"How the hell did you manage to say that with a straight face." But Senan felt that deserved a kiss – just a quick one. His bladder was reminding him there were some things he had no intention of sharing with anyone, not even his fated mate.

/~/~/~/~/

"I really missed doing this." Senan was wearing his glamor, sipping happily on his large cup of coffee. The remains of their meal were still on the table, and Finlay was feeling pretty good about life.

"Eating out?" It wasn't something Finlay did very often in his down time, but if Senan enjoyed it they could make it a regular date.

"Being out socially, yes. I think I told you, one of my favorite things to do is to be out people-watching in a social setting like this. It's always so interesting."

"In what way?" Finlay watched people, too, but they were usually paranormals he would have to apprehend for some reason or another. Somehow he didn't think that was what Senan meant.

"People on Earth are so different from those found on the fae realm. It's real here, real life. When I used to socialize in the fae world, it was like watching an elaborate theatre production. A complete act in a carefully crafted play." Senan shook his head, clearly remembering the things he saw. "Even a casual brunch like this was unheard of."

"Tell me about it...if you don't mind." Finlay chuckled softly. "Obviously, the fae realm isn't somewhere I'm likely to visit."

"Me neither." Senan nodded as Finlay winced – *Oops* - "But I've made my peace with that." He inhaled sharply and then blew it out softly. "Look at this lovely restaurant – warm, inviting, intimate, and comfortable. You can tell from the color schemes of golds and warm brown tones, with the teal and cream accents, that the owners want you to feel soothed in this space. There's nothing jarring. Nothing in this room is vying for our attention, allowing us to enjoy our food and conversation without being dominated by the space itself. Does that make sense?"

Finlay glanced around the restaurant. It was a place he was familiar with which is why he felt it was a good place to take his mate. "I never noticed the decor before, until you mentioned it. I just know I've always liked this place," he admitted quietly. "But yes, you're right. Don't they have places like this on the fae realm?"

"Ah, the infamous first date on the fae realm is nothing like this." Senan had a lovely laugh. "Picture a room...hmm for an intimate meeting like ours, the room would probably be four to six times the size of this restaurant."

"Sounds like a mini ballroom." Finlay wrinkled up his nose. He was not a fan of formal events.

"Exactly, and for this small, intimate 'getting to know your date' date, the meal will be shared with around twenty to fifty close friends. You have to understand that every date, especially in the early days of a relationship, is an opportunity to showcase wealth, connections, and how admired you are by your intimate circle."

"On a date?" Finlay couldn't believe what he was hearing, but Senan was nodding. "How do fae actually get to know each other personally if there are so many people around?"

"They don't." Senan clearly found Finlay's shock amusing. "But if you spend your life walking around as though you have a broomstick up your ass, then you really don't want someone you want to be intimate with to know about that. So they hide their flaws among a room full of people who behave in the same way they do."

Resting his elbows on the table, Finlay said, "But surely, if this dating proves successful, and I use that term loosely, but surely there's going to come a time when those two people are in bed together, with no one else around. You know, getting to know each other intimately."

"Ah, yes." Senan paused for a moment, putting down his coffee mug. "I'm not going to discuss those aspects that I've had personal experience with. I am well aware that's not the sort of thing I should mention to my protective wolf shifter mate," – *I resemble that remark* – "but I can say that the bedroom side of things ends up being a similar production, just on a smaller scale. Mostly it's a case of a lot of things said and done for effect, rather than genuine feeling."

Finlay shifted in his seat, intimate memories of his own flitting through his head. If anything, he was someone who invested too much feeling into casual encounters, usually giving others the wrong idea. "Fair enough. Moving on."

Senan laughed again and Finlay was sure some of what he was thinking must've leaked through their bond. Leaning over the table, Senan said quietly, "Did you see that older couple over by the window?"

Finlay nodded quickly. He'd scoped out everyone in the restaurant the moment they'd arrived.

"You probably ignored them, considering they weren't a threat at all, and that's understandable. A lot of older people are ignored or considered invisible in society. But if you really watch, can you see how much they love each other?" Senan sighed. "He touches her hand, they're talking softly to each other, and they've shared food off each other's plates. She laughs at his jokes, he's showing he cares with every glance. They're in their own happy bubble. In the world the way it is right now, wouldn't you agree how sweet that is?"

Finlay looked down at their empty plates. "Was I meant to share my food with you as a sign of affection?" *I might have to order double meals.*

But Senan was shaking his head. "I'm not getting between a wolf shifter and his food," he said with a chuckle. "However, I do know that if we were stuck in the woods somewhere, and I had no means of getting us food, your wolf would go off and hunt for me, making sure I was fed first. Am I right?"

"My wolf's quite keen to get us lost in the woods just so he could do something like that." Reaching across the table, Finlay took Senan's hand, stroking over his slender fingers. He could see behind the glamour. Senan was a strong man and a wonderfully unique individual – someone else that others might underestimate. "I'm hoping you'll like to meet my furry side real soon."

"We should do that this afternoon." Senan's eyes sparkled as he pointed at Finlay with his free hand. "I have never had an after-date experience like that. I'd love to."

Finlay and his wolf heard the word love, and Finlay sighed. *This man is going to wrap me around his little finger, and I'm going to love every minute of it.*

Chapter Fourteen

The first thing that struck Senan as he watched Finlay getting undressed in the forest clearing some miles out of town was how at home Finlay seemed to be in the great outdoors. Senan was feeling so much better - relaxed, happy, pleased to have a chance to share his passion for people-watching with his mate, and now it was time for him to share something that made Finlay happy as well.

"You don't have to worry about the Luna Pack," Finlay said. He pulled his shirt over his head, folded it loosely and dropped it on the hood of the car. "The pack is about thirty minutes that way." He pointed to the right. "But we're going the other way. The boundaries of the pack territory are at least a mile away from here, so we shouldn't come across any wandering pack members."

"I'm sure you'll protect me from them." Senan smiled and raised his eyebrows in an effort to hide his sudden onset of nerves. He hadn't deliberately gone anywhere near the Luna Pack ever, and just knowing he was within running distance of the territory – at least in wolf terms – didn't fill him with warm fuzzies. *I'm doing this for Finlay.*

"If there was anywhere else suitable where I could shift and run, then I would." Finlay seemed to be doing a spot of mind reading.

"It's fine." Senan wasn't lying. He understood Finlay's wolf had to stretch his legs, and there weren't that many options when it came to places he could shift and run outside of town. Senan's back garden was barely big enough to host a flower bed, and from what he'd seen at Finlay's when they went to get some clothes for him, there wasn't much room there either.

"I'm sure you know this about wolf shifters, but I should probably repeat it anyway. My wolf looks like a natural wolf, he's just a little bit bigger."

Senan chuckled. Finlay was in the process of taking off his pants. "I think everything about you is a little bit bigger than the norm, don't you?" He made a point of directing his gaze at Finlay's crotch and waggled his eyebrows.

"Gods, you shouldn't do that." But Finlay was laughing, hopping around to get his left foot out of his pants leg. "You just have to look at me, and my cock goes boing and springs to attention. My wolf wants out, and that doesn't mix with a hardon."

"I can try not looking." Senan hid his face with his hands, but then he opened his fingers so he could peep through them. "I thought shifters were fine with being naked."

"We are. I am. But you rev my motor just by looking at me. I don't usually have that issue when I shift." Finlay finally got his pants off and put them with his shirt. "Okay, just a few quick things. You know my wolf is sentient."

Senan nodded, dropping his hands so he could pay attention. Not exactly easy when his sexy mate was naked.

"My wolf knows who you are, he sees you as his precious mate, and he'll understand everything you say, even if he can't exactly talk back. I think my wolf's total range of vocalizations includes a few growls in different pitches, barking, the wolf howl of course." Finlay flicked a glance in the direction of the pack grounds. "My wolf won't be doing that today, but he's also been known to huff on occasion."

"A huffy puppy, how adorable." Senan laughed as he watched Finlay's body shimmer with magic. That magic was unique to shifters everywhere, and something that a fae, mage, or any other magic user had no hope of repeating.

Within a blink, where Finley stood, a large, black, gray, and brown wolf appeared. The first thing Senan noticed was the intelligence in his bright yellow eyes. Finlay's wolf had a healthy coat, with a wide chest. Standing still the way he was, Senan estimated the wolf's back was at least as tall as Senan's hip bone. Sort of natural. Not small. But Finlay's wolf was definitely magnificent.

"Is there a sniffing protocol for shifters when they meet their mates in their shifted form?" Moving forward Senan held out his hand, not quite sure what the wolf would do.

The wolf sniffed, licked it, and then nudged Senan's hand so that he was petting the wolf between his ears. "Ah, I see how this is going to go," Senan said, laughing quietly. "For all you looking big, fierce, and intimidating, you're really just a gorgeous fur baby that likes scritches, aren't you?"

The wolf was wagging his tail, and he had a big grin on his face. Senan had heard that term before - a wolfy grin - but now he was seeing it in the flesh, and it really was darn cute. It was clear the wolf was happy to see him, and be touched by him, and that made Senan feel a lot better about where they were.

"Did you want to go for a walk? I can walk with you for a little way, if you like. Or do you want to run off and go and sniff and do whatever it is that wolves do? I don't need you hunting me a rabbit," Senan added quickly when the wolf looked keen to take off into the woods.

"I've already had lunch so I'm not hungry. Let's make sure no innocent animals die just because you think you have to provide for me. I know you *want* to provide for me. I don't *need* you to prove it to me right now."

He got a woof for that, which made him jump, but that struck Senan as being funny as well. He'd never been in a situation where he'd ever talked to an animal, let alone talked to an animal that could actually understand him. "I'll follow you. We'll wander for a bit, and then if I get tired, I'll just sit somewhere, and you can just go run and do wolfy things."

Back before Senan got a job, he liked spending a lot of time outside. There was something very freeing about walking through an unruly garden, or patches of bush and seeing the way plants grew and adapted to their neighbors. *Another way I rebelled against the fae life.* His former friends and family preferred environments they could control.

Senan was also curious, watching the wolf in what was his natural habitat. Finlay, as a wolf, seemed to be a lot more alert than other animals that Senan had seen in videos and films. He seemed to be constantly sniffing the air, or around the bases of trees, perhaps picking up traces of other wolves. He got the distinct impression

Finlay didn't want to come across anybody from his previous pack, and frankly Senan felt the same way. *You can keep being as protective as you like.*

But as they walked along it was easy for Senan to convince himself that there were no other predators or people around for miles. The trees provided plenty of shade overhead. The air was mildly warm enough to be pleasant that Senan didn't feel he needed a coat. He would've loved to have let go of his glamour and just wander along in his natural form, complete with wings, but Finlay's caution made him hold back. He could tell just by the way the wolf was acting that Finlay wasn't as comfortable roaming lands so close to the pack as he might have been in the past.

That has to be because of his brother. Letting Finlay pick their trail, Senan thought back to when Finlay had pulled out his card to pay for their meal at the restaurant. His card was attached to the back of his phone and when that came out of his pocket, Senan had caught a glimpse of the screen. There were at least twelve messages and missed calls all from the one number. As Senan hadn't heard any dings or notification bells while they were eating he could only assume that Finlay had his phone on silent.

Morgan. It had to be. If it had been anyone else leaving that many messages or calls, all from the same number, then Senan was sure Finlay would've at least read the messages. Finlay had an important job. Keeping his phone on silent probably wasn't allowed if Finlay typically got called into work. Senan got another warm fuzzy feeling, knowing that Finlay was genuinely making an effort to focus on him for their first day, but the sheer number of attempts at contact concerned him.

I can't think why Morgan wants to get in touch so badly anyway. Senan believed Finlay when he said he'd cut his ties with the pack. His mate didn't lie. It made sense to Senan that if Morgan was still trying to get in touch with Finlay, despite his mate not being part of his pack anymore, then it had to be because of Senan.

It's not like you can tell me, running around on all fours. Senan smiled at the wolf who was loping along ahead of him, his tail waving like a flag, his head going in all directions. *And I did shut down Finlay's conversations about his brother the two times he tried to talk to me about it, so I don't have anyone else to blame for that than myself.*

Finlay barked, and Senan looked up, glancing around - not that his magic could sense anything at all beyond the natural wildlife that was supposed to be in a forest area. "What's up? Is something bothering you? If you need to run, you know I can't keep up with you. But I can sit here if you like." He pointed to a fallen tree that provided a perfect bench seat. "I'll just perch my butt on here, and you go do whatever it is you need to do. My magic will be able to sense you, and I know you won't go far."

The wolf seemed undecided, looking at Senan who did go and sit down, and then looking out in the direction of where Senan knew the pack grounds were. "You go and check for intruders. I'll be fine here on my own. I've got my phone so I can listen to some music or read a book while you're gone." He wagged his finger at the wolf who was listening intently. "Just don't forget me and leave me here because I'm not sure I know how to get back to the car without just translocating to it."

The big wolf bounded over, sniffing at Senan's chest, and then rubbing his head on it. Senan gave his ears another rub. "Go on, I'll be fine." After another sniff, the wolf bounded off and disappeared into the bushes. Senan tugged at his shirt and sniffed the material. "Did he just scent mark me? I thought that was what cats did."

Giggling at the mental image of an offended looking wolf shifter who would probably hate being compared to a cat, Senan pulled out his phone, seeing a message from Gabby. After replying to her that, yes, he and Finlay would be at his place later, Senan went into his reading app and clicked on a book he hadn't finished yet. Yawning, he settled his butt a bit more firmly on the log and started to read.

Chapter Fifteen

It was about ten minutes later when Senan looked up from his phone screen when he heard a rustling in the bushes across from the clearing where he was sitting. A long nose peeked out and then a wolf appeared. At first glance, Senan thought it was Finlay. But his magic, which always seemed to be a better judge of things than his eyes, quickly identified that the wolf wasn't his mate, in which case there was a good chance the wolf he was looking at was Alpha Morgan.

The strange wolf had similar coloring to Finlay, but as Senan looked more closely, he could see that the new wolf had a patch of brown on his chest, whereas Finlay's was more on his shoulders, and Finlay had a gray tuft of hair on his forehead, which the strange wolf didn't have. The wolf didn't have the same bulk as Finlay had and might have been an inch shorter at the shoulder.

This has to be Morgan. Any other shifter would've just carried on by and not even let me see them.

Deciding he really didn't want to talk to Morgan or any wolf except Finlay, Senan just ignored the animal, who had now made his way into the clearing. He knew enough about shifter culture to know that he was in no danger from the strange wolf. The animal trying to stare him down wasn't a natural creature, he was definitely a shifter. Senan's magic picked up the buzz of the magic a shifter used to enable his shift, and besides, the eyes had too much awareness to belong to a frightened, curious, or attacking animal. This wolf was looking at him as though he knew who Senan was.

Shifters were bound by shifter law and could absolutely not attack any person on two legs, or even another shifter unless there was a clear and obvious threat involved. Senan wasn't on pack territory – he knew darn well Finlay wouldn't have led him onto pack grounds. No one owned the patch of grass with its dead log he was sitting on, meaning Senan was well within his rights to sit there.

That meant Senan could ignore the wolf as much as he was ignoring the squirrel who was chattering two trees over. The squirrel was probably worried Senan was going after his nut stash. He looked back down at his screen and carried on reading. He was enjoying the story.

Senan heard a deep rumble after just a few moments. It would seem the wolf, much like Alpha Morgan, didn't like being ignored. Senan checked on his magic levels. He'd been doing really well since Finlay had come into his life. He was still bubbling from the night before, despite having maintained his glamor for more than four hours.

Without bothering to look at the wolf, Senan warded his glamour, setting up a protective bubble around himself, roughly a foot away from his skin. Finlay would be able to touch him through it because they were mates. Morgan, or any other shifter could not.

The wolf was getting closer, and either he had a facial tick, or he was trying out different expressions as if hoping one might work. First there was the intimidating stance – ears back, teeth showing – nothing like the wolfy grin Finlay had. That was the face of a wolf who was saying "Hey, this is my land, and you have no right to be here."

Senan knew that he did, so he just ignored him.

Coming closer still, just two small steps at a time, the wolf's expression changed. This time he had his head slightly tilted, although he was still watching Senan intently. *Is this your curiosity era?* Senan had no idea and didn't want to know.

Although... it was getting really difficult for Senan not to say anything. Thinking logically, meeting up with Morgan – assuming that was who the wolf was – was inevitable. He was now mated to the man's brother and while Senan wasn't sure why the Fates thought that was a good idea, the claim was done. He just didn't want to be dealing with Morgan, or any other wolf for that matter, on the first day after he'd been claimed.

It might be time for you to make a heroic appearance, Fin, Senan thought, although as fast as he thought it, he hoped that wouldn't be the case. If Fin fought the wolf – brother or not – the outcome wasn't likely to be good for them as a mated couple. There was no way Senan wanted to deal with the Shifter Council again if he could help it.

I'll just keep reading and with luck, the nuisance will go away.

Of course, because he was being a nuisance, the wolf didn't go away. No, the damn wolf shifted, and all Senan could think when he saw Morgan in the flesh, was that his mind had played tricks on him – now he knew Finlay, he could see that Morgan only had a passing resemblance in terms of coloring and height to his mate.

Ho-hum. Much like he had at the bar all those years ago, Senan stayed where he was. He told Finlay he would sit on the log, and he would sit on the log until Finlay came by to collect him, or he decided he wanted to leave.

"I didn't expect to see you in my part of the forest." Alpha Morgan didn't sound any less cocky than he did the night that Senan had met him.

"This is not pack land. Finlay made sure of that." Senan said, not even looking at him although he bookmarked the page he was reading and closed the app. "I'm not in your territory. Leave me alone."

"Where's Finlay? He said you and he were fated. I've been calling and messaging him for a week and he's not responding."

"You've been texting and messaging him since last Friday night, and if he hasn't responded then I'm guessing he doesn't want to talk to you. I don't want to talk to you either. People have the right to decide that for themselves and expect to have that decision respected." Senan checked his notifications. Gabby was coming around and wanted to know if Finlay liked pizza. *He's a wolf shifter. I think they will eat almost anything. But double the order.* He hit send and noticed Morgan was glaring now, his fists clenched.

"There's no point in standing there posturing. You're a bald-faced liar and a coward in my opinion. I have the scars to prove it. I won't waste my attention on anybody who would behave in such a dishonorable fashion as you did."

"Is that what you told Finlay? Is that why my brother won't have anything to do with me?"

"There you go again, rewriting history. Finlay walked away from you before he claimed me. I've got nothing to do with what you two get up to. My relationship is with Finlay, not with you."

Had Finlay known Morgan would show up? If he had, surely he would've come sprinting to Senan's side the moment Morgan shifted. *Or has he been waylaid by other wolves causing a diversion?* Senan strained his ears, but he couldn't hear anyone fighting. But then his hearing wasn't as sharp as a shifter's was.

We might have to leave town if this is going to become a habit every time Finlay wants to shift. But even as he thought that he got angry all over again. Senan had rebuilt his life, and he was happy. Finlay was happy. Morgan was the only one who wasn't happy, and Senan couldn't give two fucks about that.

"Why won't you talk to me?" Morgan demanded.

This time Senan looked up, meeting the man's eyes without flinching. "I don't fucking want to. Now piss off and leave me alone."

Morgan seemed to collapse in on himself – his shoulders slumped, his fists unclenched, and Senan was sure the man's expression was one of confusion. He'd clearly gotten so used to being treated as the Alpha, as somebody that everybody else bowed down to, he really didn't know what to do when somebody challenged him on anything.

And Senan wasn't even challenging him. He was speaking his truth. Something he should have done four years ago. Something he thought he had done four years ago. But something he was perfectly capable of doing now. They weren't in a public space. There was no danger of anybody else getting hurt. He would protect himself if he had to, but Senan was damned sure that Alpha Morgan would never get the chance to hurt him again.

"You... You..." Morgan was reduced to spluttering. "My brother is my heir. He has to talk to me."

"Your brother *was* your heir." Senan still didn't look away, and he could actually see the point where Morgan was struggling to hold his eyes. Maybe it was the scar on his face, which, in his human glamour looked very thin. But it was still there, or maybe it was because Morgan knew what it looked like underneath. It could be that Morgan wasn't used to anybody meeting his eyes in the first place, meeting him as an equal. And for the first time since he'd gotten his scar, that's how Senan felt.

I'm not afraid of him anymore. Standing up, Senan made sure his wards were in place while he dropped his glamour. His wings, thank goodness, stayed against his back the way they should, but Senan could see from Morgan's eyes that the passing of time had lessened his memory, too. He blinked away his shirt and, with a single finger, traced the line of his jagged scar from the corner of his eye, down his cheek, underneath his lips, and then a full slash from the edge of his neck to his underarm. Morgan seemed hypnotized by the motion.

"You marked me," Senan said quietly. "I am forbidden, under the clauses in the punishment you insisted on, to heal myself. I will wear these scars until the end of my existence, because of your lies. I lost my home and family. I lost my position in my realm and my status as a member of the Fae Court. But I'm still standing.

"Hear my vow, Alpha Morgan. I will not engage with you in any way, shape, or form, for any reason until my scars heal and are no longer visible."

"But you just said you can't..."

Senan nodded. "That's right. I can't." He moved his finger, tapping his newly formed mating scar left by Finlay on his neck the night before. Morgan's eyes widened. "Your brother marked me, too. Because of this scar, your brother won't have anything to do with you again, either. You brought this on yourself, Alpha Morgan. You'll have to live with it, the same as I had to."

And then, because he wanted to and he could, Senan translocated himself back to Finlay's car. His wolf would find him. He had no doubt about that. If Morgan tracked him there, then Senan could just close and lock the doors and windows. He could easily ignore him from there as well, and the car seats were more comfortable than a log.

/~/~/~/~/

Senan hadn't even finished another chapter of his book when Finlay came sprinting out of the trees, naked, heading for the car. Swiping his clothes, still on the hood, Finlay barely managed to get his pants on, before he was yanking open the driver's door, cursing and swearing as he slumped in the seat.

"Those fucking bastards...those no-good fleabag, simpering sycophants, pieces of shit!" He had dirt on his cheek, his hair was all over the place, and the beginnings of what looked like a bruise on his rib cage.

"Did you have a nice meeting with some of your pack bros, mate of mine?" Senan put his phone back in his pocket.

Finlay whirled around in his seat, his elbows resting on his seat back and the steering wheel. "They were a diversion, a fucking diversion. I didn't know Morgan could be such a fucking asshole. I smelled him in the clearing, where I left you. He could've hurt you and I couldn't get back to you. Are you sure you're all right?"

Ah. Senan had been right. Morgan wasn't stupid, just devious. "I'm fine. Really good actually. Did you kill anyone?"

"No!"

"Well done. We don't want any issues with the Shifter Council so soon into our mating. I'm proud of you." Leaning across the center console, Senan stretched his torso, placing his lips on Finlay's angry ones. Pressing just hard enough to make an impact, Senan sat back in his seat and sighed. "Gabby is bringing us pizza for dinner. I told her to double our typical order. I hope you like Maximus Khan movies."

"That's all you have to say?" Finlay was stroking over his lip where Senan had kissed him.

"Yep. I told Morgan I wouldn't talk to him again until my scars had healed. I also mentioned that you wouldn't have anything to do with him until that time either. Sound good?"

Finlay was clearly stunned. "But your scars... Ah. Yes. Brilliant." His harried face broke into a smile. "I would've told him the same thing if I'd thought about it."

"Perfect. So now we need to get home, mate of mine. If we get back soon enough, we'll have time to shower together before Gabby comes around for dinner. You're decidedly grubby."

Finlay wasn't a silly man either. Senan smiled and closed his eyes as the car sped back to town. He thought he could hear a wolf howling as they left, but as Finlay didn't say anything about it, neither did he.

Chapter Sixteen

"How are you feeling?" Senan sounded sleepy, and Finlay wasn't surprised.

"Your friend Gabby is a force of nature." Finlay chuckled. "Does she always do a 'whoop-whoop' every time she sees a man take a shirt off in a movie?"

"Ah, not just any man." Senan snuggled against Finlay's chest, his breathing slow and relaxed. "Only Maximus Khan has caused that reaction, so far. I don't know what she'd ever do if she ever met him."

"Hmm. I could probably arrange that." Brushing a kiss on Senan's hair, Finlay added, "Do you think she'd like that?"

"Like it?" Senan lurched up, his hands resting on Finlay's chest, his hair spilling over his shoulders as his eyes widened. "Gabby would adopt you if she thought you could do that. You'd become family. Everyone else in her life would cease to exist. She would be fussing over you with baked goods and endless beers every time she saw you if you facilitated a meeting with her amazing movie star."

"I'm quite partial to baked goods and endless beers." Finlay started laughing. "But my gods, wouldn't it be funny if she met him and didn't like him? I mean, he's a nice enough guy, really friendly, but when she sees him in the movie, he's playing a character – that's not the real person. In real life, he scratches his ass the same as the rest of us."

"I wouldn't see that as a bad thing." Senan snuggled back down on Finlay's chest again. "There's not a person in Gabby's existence who doesn't know about her infatuation with Maximus Khan. If she did meet him and didn't like him as a personality, then she might turn her attraction to someone else, which would mean we could watch some of the newer movies that have come out that don't star Maximus Khan."

"He's only done about ten movies."

"I know." Senan yawned. "And I could probably recite the words to every one of them thanks to her."

As Finlay looked down, he could see Senan watching his face.

"You know I was actually talking about the situation with your brother, and the Luna Pack this afternoon when I asked if you were all right."

"I guessed that. Gabby was easier to talk about." Finlay thought for a moment. In the calm of Senan's bedroom, with his mate in his arms and the smell of their shared lovemaking in the air, the events of the afternoon seemed a lifetime away.

"Today was a real eye-opener for me. That's the only way I can put it. My own brother sent four of his strongest betas after me, not to hurt me, but to distract me long enough so he could get to you.

"What type of an asshole Alpha does that to his pack mates? He had to know I could beat them – they weren't allowed to hurt me, so he was putting them at a disadvantage for a start. The second I knew what was happening, my only thought was to get back to you, and they kept getting in my way.

"UGH, it makes me so angry. Morgan should never treat his pack mates like that, but he was just so hellbent on getting his own way. It was pure selfishness. One of the betas told me they'd been there every day since Friday night, waiting for me to go for a run. Who does that?"

"You answered that yourself, hon. He's always been selfish." Senan's hand stroking over his chest reminded Finlay of what and who was important. "Did you speak to him at all before you came to find me?"

"Nope." Finlay blew out a long breath. "I ran back to the clearing. You weren't there. I remembered what you'd said about translocating to the car, and I could smell your magic in the air. I could also scent Morgan who had gone in the opposite direction. For me, the choice was obvious." Finlay chuckled again. "There you were sitting in the car, reading on your phone as happy as you please. While I probably looked like the wild man of the woods."

"Your wolf got plenty of exercise." Senan yawned again. "I guess what's worrying me more is what happens now? Do we have to move, or find you somewhere else to shift? Because, no disrespect to your only family member, but I know I really don't want your brother popping up in our lives like a stinking turd every five minutes."

"I don't think he will." Cradling his mate close, Finlay said quietly, "What you did, what you said, the way you said it, and everything else, I'm so damn proud of you for standing up for yourself. But you also proved to Morgan that the only way he can get his own way with us will probably lose him his position as Alpha. And being Alpha of the Luna Pack was all Morgan's wanted since he was eight years old."

"Then he's got what he wanted. It's been four years since I first saw him, and it's not like I've bumped into him since then... Not until you came barging into my space."

"Meeting you was the only decent thing to come out of that event, and ironically, the only reason I was there as Morgan's plus one, was because the man can't get a date."

"We both know why. You can send him a book on dating tips for Christmas." Senan's body was warm against Finlay's side, and his cock twitched. "Hmm, when I'm curled up with you, the thought of working as many shifts as I've been used to does not appeal."

"Great minds think alike." Finlay trailed his hand over Senan's shoulder. "I think I'll get in touch with my boss and let him know I'll only be available for local work. The jobs will be few and far between, but today, that panic I felt at not being able to get to you was very real. Not that I think you can't look after yourself, because you clearly can, but…yeah. I suppose that sounds lame."

"Sounds like a mate talking to me. But we might need a new house. We need somewhere for you to have a grill, and I don't even have a back porch."

Finlay had already decided to put his house on the market. Senan's was smaller, but it was a lovely space, perfect for the two of them. "I'll get in touch with your landlord tomorrow and see if he wants to sell. Then I can build us a porch for the grill."

"Now that's a sexy image." Senan giggled against his chest. "You shirtless with tight jeans and a tool belt. Hmm. My favorite fictional fantasy. I do love a man who's good with his hands."

"Ooh, you'll have to show me some of the books you've been reading." Finlay pulled his mate so Senan was lying on his chest. "Did you want me to show you how good I am with my...hammer?"

"I can't believe how well you say things like that with such a straight face." Senan was still laughing when Finlay pulled him in for a kiss.

Epilogue

Three months later

"Jeffrey's leg is still in a cast." Gabby rolled half over in her chair, she was laughing so hard. "And the thing is, if you ask him how he did it, his story gets more and more elaborate every time. Betty told me in strictest confidence that he'd tripped over a rope at that Shibari thing. He was so busy eyeing up all the displays, he didn't pay any attention to where he was going."

Senan laughed with her. There were a few times he missed working, but Gabby made sure he didn't lose his friendships just because he'd rather spend his time with his mate. Looking across their new porch, he caught Finlay's eyes and winked. His mate looked very competent cooking meat on his new grill and chatting to Brennan and Alex. A couple of Finlay's shifter friends had dropped in and were entertaining Fern and Aisha. The only one who hadn't arrived was Wyatt, but he had an exam and would be dropping by later.

For Senan, life had become fun again. He wasn't sure when it happened exactly, but with Finlay in his life, he found himself laughing more, more willing to go out, or even just lay around and enjoy his books – and his mate. He didn't worry if his scar or fae self was showing. Finlay accepted him, and for Senan that was a confidence boost he didn't realize he needed.

"So...how are things with you?" Gabby tapped his arm. "Is mated life all it's cracked up to be?"

"Yes." Senan nodded. "It's...life changing in the most amazing way."

"Here's hoping it happens to me one day. Surely there's a shifter out there somewhere who can handle all my awesomeness. Oh, my gods, did I tell you about that last date I went on? I thought things were going so well over dinner, and then he started telling me about how his wife didn't understand him. His wife! I got out of that restaurant like my ass was on fire. He'd never mentioned a wife when we were making plans to meet up. I tell you, there are times when I just want to give up... Oh, my gods. Why didn't you tell me?"

"Tell you what?" Senan got up and looked around as Gabby started screaming and flapping her arms around. His eyes widened as a new man went over to Finlay, embracing him warmly. A very familiar-looking man, although he was wearing more clothes than the last time Senan had seen him. "I didn't know. I swear I didn't know."

Finlay must've said something as he and the new arrival came over. "Senan, a friend of mine was in town. I hope you don't mind him dropping in. Maximus, this is my mate, Senan and his good friend, Gabby."

"It's an honor to meet you, Senan." Maximus Khan gave him a brief nod, but Senan could already see his attention was more focused on Gabby who was now burying her face in her shaking hands.

"I'm going to kill you. I'm going to stab you with my fingernails for this, Senan. How could you not tell me?"

"Excuse me, beautiful lady, are you all right?"

Gabby looked up, her red curls flying as she nodded. "Beautiful? You... You're Maximus Khan. In my friend's backyard – a friend who didn't tell me you were coming. Maximus Khan!"

"And you, my lovely lady smell delicious." Maximus's voice got deeper, and Senan saw his eyes flash with his animal side. "You're the mate I've waited for my whole life. We must get to know each other. Excuse us, Fin, Senan, nice barbecue."

Before Gabby or Senan could say another word, Maximus picked Gabby up out of her chair and carried her bridal style around the side of the house. Senan just heard a faint, "I'll call you tomorrow..." before the sound was drowned out by a car door slamming.

"So, he's not one for conversation, is he?" Senan started to laugh. "Did you set him up to do that?"

"No, I wouldn't do that." Finlay quickly shook his head. "I just let him know we were having a small get-together, and it would be a good opportunity for him to meet you. If he says Gabby is his mate, then she definitely is. Shifters don't joke about things like that."

"Wow. Just wow." Senan poked Finlay's arm. "Your meat's burning."

"Damn it, Brennan, you were supposed to turn it over. Haven't you seen a movie star before?" Finlay hurried over to his prized grill as Wyatt came around the side of the house.

"Hey, Senan, I think I've been hit by your magic." He was rubbing his head. "Or I could be tired." Like the rest of his friends, Wyatt had accepted Senan being a fae with no problems at all.

"Why... What did you see?" Senan only had his wards around the house, and they were set very low so his non-para friends wouldn't be impacted by them.

Wyatt pointed back in the direction he'd arrived. "I would swear I just saw Gabby being driven off in this huge limo being driven by that actor fella, Maximus Khan. I'm seeing things that aren't there, right?"

"Oh, nope. That happened. Finlay knows Maximus, and he dropped in, got one sniff of Gabby, and carried her off into the sunset. They're fated mates."

"Cool." Wyatt nodded. "That would explain why she was always going on about him without his shirt on. Hey, Aisha, how did you do on your exam?"

He wandered off and Senan sat back down watching his mate and friends enjoy each other's company. As he took a sip of the wine Finlay had brewed for them personally, he spared a thought for the family and friends he thought he had back on the fae realm. *I really don't miss them at all.*

He idly rubbed the scar on his face, no longer hidden because his friends and mate accepted him for who he truly was.

"Sen, babe, I don't think even your magic can save this steak. Do you mind having chicken instead?"

"You're the one who likes to eat your meat darn near raw. Bring it over. It's probably perfect for me." *Just like you are.* And with the smile Finlay gave him, Senan knew he was thinking the same thing.

The End

About the Author

Lisa Oliver lives in the wilds of New Zealand, although her beautiful dogs Hades and Zeus are now living somewhere else far more remote than she is. Reports indicate they truly enjoy chasing possums although they still can't catch them. In the meantime, Lisa is living a lot closer to all her adult kids and grandchildren which means she gets a lot more visitors. However, it doesn't look like she's ever going to stop writing - with over a hundred paranormal MM (and MMM) titles to her name so far, she shows no signs of slowing down.

When Lisa is not writing, she is usually reading with a cup of tea always at hand. Her grown children and grandchildren sometimes try and pry her away from the computer and have found that the best way to do it is to promise her chocolate. Lisa will do anything for chocolate… and occasionally crackers. She has also started working out, because of the chocolate and the crackers.

Lisa loves to hear from her readers and other writers (I really do, lol). You can catch up with her on any of the social media links below.

I finally got my Patreon page up and running – you can check that out at https://www.patreon.com/LisaOliver

Facebook –
http://www.facebook.com/lisaoliverauthor

Official Author page –
https://www.facebook.com/LisaOliverManloveAuthor/

My private teaser group -
https://www.facebook.com/groups/540361549650663/

My MeWe Group -
http://mewe.com/join/lisa_olivers_paranormal_pack

And Instagram -
https://www.instagram.com/lisa_oliver_author/

My blog - http://www.paranormalgayromance.com

Email me directly at yoursintuitively@gmail.com.

Other Books By Lisa Oliver

Please note, I have now marked the books that contain mpreg and MMM for those of you who don't like to read those type of stories, or for those who prefer them ☺ Completed series are now marked with an asterisk next to the series title. Hope that helps ☺

Cloverleah Pack*

Book 1 – The Reluctant Wolf – Kane and Shawn

Book 2 – The Runaway Cat – Griff and Diablo

Book 3 – When No Doesn't Cut It – Damien and Scott

Book 3.5 – Never Go Back – Scott and Damien's Trip and a free story about Malacai and Elijah

Book 4 – Calming the Enforcer – Troy and Anton

Book 5 – Getting Close to the Omega – Dean and Matthew

Book 6 – Fae for All – Jax, Aelfric and Fafnir (M/M/M)

Book 7 – Watching Out for Fangs –Josh and Vadim

Book 8 – Tangling with Bears – Tobias, Luke, and Kurt (M/M/M)

Book 9 – Angel in Black Leather – Adair and Vassago

Book 9.5 – Scenes from Cloverleah – four short stories featuring the men we've come to love

Book 10 – On the Brink – Teilo, Raff and Nereus (M/M/M)

Book 11 – Don't Tempt Fate – Marius and Cathair

Book 12 – My Treasure to Keep – Thomas and Ivan

Book 13 – Home is Where the Heart is – Wesley and Castor

The Gods Made Me Do It (Cloverleah spin off series)

Book One - Get Over It – Madison and Sebastian's story

Book Two - You've Got to be Kidding – Poseidon and Claude (mpreg)

Book Three – Don't Fight It – Lasse and Jason

Book Four – Riding the Storm – Thor and Orin (mpreg elements [Jason from previous book gives birth in this one])

Book Five – I Can See You – Artemas and Silvanus (mpreg elements – Thor gives birth in this one)

Book Six – Someone to Hold Me – Hades and Ali (mpreg elements but no birth)

Book Seven – You'll Know in Your Heart – Baby and Owen (mpreg)

Book Eight – Worth It – Zeus and Paulie (mpreg)

Book Nine – When Three Points Collide – Ra, Kirill and Arvyn (M/M/M) (mpreg elements, no birth)

Book Ten – Special Enough – Odin and Evan

Book Eleven – Reconciliation: Seth's Story – Seth and Luka (mpreg is a small part of this story)

Book Twelve – Being Loki - Loki and Anubis

Book Thirteen – Give Me A Reason – Helios and Bruno

Book Fourteen – Fenrir's Fate – Fenrir and Dorian

Book Fifteen – Wanting to Belong – Hephaestus and Landyn

Book Sixteen – Strawberries to Share: Ares' Story – Ares and Marty (mpreg)

The Necromancer's Smile* (This is a trilogy series under the name The Necromancer's Smile where the main couple, Dakar and Sy are the focus of all three books – these cannot be read as standalone).

Book One – Dakar and Sy – The Meeting

Book Two – Dakar and Sy – Family affairs

Book Three – Dakar and Sy – Taking Care of Business

Bound and Bonded Series*

Book One – Don't Touch – Levi and Steel

Book Two – Topping the Dom – Pearson and Dante

Book Three – Total Submission – Kyle and Teric

Book Four – Fighting Fangs – Ace and Devin

Book Five – No Mate of Mine – Roger and Cam

Book Six – Undesirable Mate – Phillip and Kellen

Stockton Wolves Series*

Book One – Get off My Case – Shane and Dimitri

Book Two – Copping a Lot of Sin – Ben, Sin and Gabriel (M/M/M)

Book Three – Mace's Awakening – Mace and Roan

Book Four – Don't Bite – Trent and Alexi

Book Five – Tell Me the Truth – Captain Reynolds and Nico (mpreg)

Alpha and Omega Series*

Book One – The Biker's Omega – Marly and Trent

Book Two – Dance Around the Cop – Zander and Terry

Book Three – Change of Plans - Q and Sully

Book Four – The Artist and His Alpha – Caden and Sean

Book Five – Harder in Heels – Ronan and Asaph

Book Six – A Touch of Spring – Bronson and Harley

Book Seven – If You Can't Stand the Heat – Wyatt and Stone (Previously published in an anthology)

Book Eight – Fagin's Folly – Fagin and Cooper

Book Nine – The Cub and His Alphas – Daniel, Zeke and Ty (MMM)

Book Ten – The One Thing Money Can't Buy – Cari and Quaid

Book Eleven – Precious Perfection – Devyn and Rex

Book Twelve – More Than a Handful - Karl and Tanner

Spin off from The Biker's Omega – BBQ, Bikes, and Bears – Clive and Roy

Balance – Angels and Demons*

The Viper's Heart – Raziel and Botis

Passion Punched King – Anael and Zagan

Soul Deep – Uriel and Haures

Found – Raphael and Seir

Demon Masks and Angel Wings – Michael and Orobas

Love Before Time – Lucifer and Gabriel

Arrowtown*

A Tiger's Tale – Ra and Seth (mpreg)

Snake Snack – Simon and Darwin (mpreg)

Liam's Lament – Liam Beau and Trent (MMM) (Mpreg)

Doc's Deputy – Deputy Joe and Doc (Mpreg)

Cam's Chance – Cam and Fergus (Mpreg)

Stone Cold Obsidian – Dian and Kee (Mpreg)

Brutus's Surprise – Brutus and Heath

Hal's Silence – Hal and Blade (mpreg although not the main focus of the story)

Ness's Wait – Ness and Cyrus (mpreg)

The Devil on My Chest – Rocky and Mal (mpreg)

City Dragons

Dragon's Heat – Dirk and Jon

Dragon's Fire – Samuel and Raoul

Dragon's Tears – Byron and Ivak

The Magic Users of Greenford – a new trilogy*

Book One - Illuminate

Book Two – Eradicate

Book Three – Validate

Words Not Necessary – Rocky and Neo – a spin off short story from this world.

My Arranged Marriage Fantasy Romance Books (not Fated Mates)

The Infidelity Clause – Nikolas and Caspian

Don't Judge A Prince by his Undergarments – Mintyn and Syrius

An Article of Lies – Xavier and Remy

The Pirate's Treasure – Rojan and Petrov

A Marriage of Necessity – Jasper and Avalon

Six Types of Apology – Vincent and Orion

The Gentlemen's Agreement – Serron, Patin and Jaq (MMM)

The Most Unsuitable Prince – Rupert and Winter (coming soon)

Quirk of Fate

Summons – Edward and Mammon

Reggie's Reasons – Reggie and Dirkin

The Mating of Blind Billy Hipp – Billy and Dathan

Demon Dabbling – Zese and Percy

Quirk of Fates Shorts

Saving Moses – Tucker and Moses

Catching Damont – Damont and Rebel

Not A Typical Meet Cute – Locryn and Zac

Scar Bonds: The scars that bind us – Senan and Finlay

Hellhound Collar Series

Collar and Scruff (Prequel) – Raoul and Jason

Better Than Sweets (Book 1) – Java and Cyril

Precious Blue (Book 2) – Beau and Blue (mpreg elements in last chapter.)

Cain's Shadow – Cain and Ollie (mpreg)

Cooking With Magic – Faron and Patrick

Imperfect Bonds: Kolton's story – Kolton and Simon (mpreg – sort of – has a twist)

Magical Beast – Giorgio and Enda

Assassin's Alley

Not that Kind of Demon – Python and Cyrus

Sweet Things for a Crocodile – Storm and Pax

Benedict and Bear Duology

Benedict and Bear #1 – Benedict and Dixon

Benedict and Bear #2 – What's Done is Done

The Psychic and the Vampire

The Psychic and the Vampire #1 – Ant and Viktor

The Psychic and the Vampire #2 – Ant and Viktor (coming soon)

Tangled Tentacles – in Collaboration with JP Sayle*

Book one – Alexi – Alexi and Danik

Book 2 – Victor – Azim and Victor (mpreg)

Book 3 – Todd – Todd, Lucas, and Ki – MMM (mpreg)

Book 4 – Markov – Markov and Cassius

Book 5 – Kelvin – Kelvin and Magnus (mpreg - Markov)

Assassins To Order With JP Sayle*

Marvin – Marvin and Ajani

Ben – Ben, Nico, and Teilo (MMM)

The Baby Question – a short story catching up with men from the Tangled Tentacles and Assassin series (MM, MMM and Mpreg)

Duron – Duron and Beaumont

Conrad – Conrad and Kylo (mpreg elements)

Dancing With The Devil – Wyatt and James (mpreg)

Demon Obsession Series with JP Sayle*

Demon Obsession – Dakata and Silas

The Controller's Obsession – Merihem and Peni (mpreg)

The Secretary's Obsession – Scott and George (mpreg)

The King's Obsession – Asmodeus and Dougal (mpreg)

Standalone:

I Should've Stayed Home: Irwin's Story – Part of the Nocturne Bay collab series – Irwin and Kolton

The Fall of the Fairy Tale Prince – Charlie and Lex (A spin off from Dancing Around the Cop and Change of Plans in the A&O series)

Stay True to Me – Con and Ven

Rowan and the Wolf – Rowan and Shadow

Bound by Blood – Max and Lyle – (a spin off from Cloverleah Pack #7)

The Power of the Bite – Dax and Zane

One Wrong Step – Robert and Syron

Uncaged – Carlin and Lucas (Shifter's Uprising in conjunction with Thomas Oliver)

Also under the penname Lee Oliver/Lisa Oliver

Northern States Pack Series*

Book One – Ranger's End Game – Ranger and Aiden

Book Two – Cam's Promise – Cam and Levi

Book Three – Under Sean's Protection – Sean and Kyle

Book Four – Newton's Law – Newton and Tron

Made in the USA
Columbia, SC
01 July 2025